SECOND LIFE

PAUL GRINER

SECOND

LIFE

A NOVEL

SOFT SKULL PRESS

Library of Congress Cataloging-in-Publication Data

Griner, Paul.
   Second life : a novel / Paul Griner.
      pages ; cm
   ISBN 978-1-61902-480-9 (hardcover : acid-free paper)
1. Dead--Fiction. 2. Organ trafficking--Fiction. 3. Medical fiction. I. Title.
   PS3557.R5314S43 2015
   813'.54--dc23
                              2014033798

ISBN 978-1-61902-480-9

Cover design by Charles Brock, Faceout Studios
Interior Design by Tabitha Lahr

Soft Skull Press
An Imprint of COUNTERPOINT
2560 Ninth Street, Suite 318
Berkeley, CA 94710
www.softskull.com

Printed in the United States of America
Distributed by Publishers Group West

10 9 8 7 6 5 4 3 2 1

For Laura, Paul, and Clara Hill

You are a little soul carrying around a corpse.
—Epictetus

My soul-bird loves my body-cage only when it is kept fit, pure, and absolutely immaculate.
—Sri Chinmoy, *Ten Thousand Flower-Flames*

1

Her body is missing.

What? I said, still waking up, the darkness humming around me. I shifted the phone to my other ear, thinking I'd misheard.

Lia's body, it's missing, Mrs. Stefanini said. Can you help, Elena? Please?

The normal question would be, How does a body go missing? But I'd been in the business long enough to know that bodies often did. Once someone died, all kinds of things could happen. After the family left, if there was family, a nurse or an attendant took the body down to the morgue on a service elevator so the public wouldn't see it, an understandable sleight of hand. Commendable, even.

The body was trundled off to the morgue in a mostly silent last walk, signed in, and left. The diener had it then, and I'd been a diener, so I knew the routines that followed.

The paperwork, the cleaning of the body, the autopsy and the phone calls: to an undertaker, if one had been specified, to the coroner, if there'd been a crime, to the med school, if interns and med students needed to practice intubation and catheterization. To the body brokers, if the body wasn't claimed.

None of that for Lia, it seemed, save perhaps the body broker.

Still, I was surprised that Mrs. Stefanini had called. I hadn't known that Lia was dead, for one thing, and I hadn't heard from the Stefaninis for three years, and the last time I had, Mrs. Stefanini herself told me never to call again.

Now, her voice unnaturally loud in the dark, she said, She crashed on the other side of the river and they brought her back to operate. Then she disappeared. We can't find her. Won't you please help? I can't go through this another time.

It was crossing the river that gave rise to my memories of body brokering. How many bodies had I ferried across it myself? Victims of car and motorcycle accidents, gunshots both intentional and accidental, strokes, drownings, poisonings, hangings and domestic violence, old age and cancer, ruptured veins, failed kidneys, bad hearts.

The list was nearly endless, sometimes peculiar (one man who drank too much water), usually predictable (people who drank too much alcohol), occasionally piercing (a child who drank a gallon of blue antifreeze, thinking it Kool-Aid), but ultimately numbing, because as their numbers climbed, your sensitivity lessened and your connection to life altered in ways even now you don't fully understand.

You began to think you carried with you everywhere the scent of the dead, a taint that even a savage scrubbing couldn't remove, and that made you more than mildly paranoid, so that you went out less often. The rare times you did meet someone it was only for a quick hook-up, and even then it was easy to note their skin tone and study their limbs, thinking of them as product. Tibias first, then the fibula, long and lean and lucrative, and the spine, the spine, the golden spine, which, as you ran your fingers up the knobs of some stray companion, making your temporary bedmate shiver, made it nearly impossible not to calculate cost and profit, or how you'd peel their skin and bag it, since those long, smoked-salmon colored strips of skin came at such a premium, $1,000 per square foot. How you told the dead you were about to harvest that this was a good thing, as if they might understand you.

It came back so easily, though that was partly due to the time and the call: two AM and the name on the caller ID; I almost hadn't answered, thinking Mrs. Stefanini might be drunk and angry, lashing out. She wouldn't be the first, only the most personal, but I was glad I'd had the fortitude to answer once I heard what she wanted, and then ashamed I was still making this about me.

Lia. Lia was gone, which seemed impossible.

My throat thickened, but I cleared it and said, Of course I'll help, ignoring the voice in my head shouting, *You're still on probation* (Lia's voice, really, as she had always been better at warning me off my various stupidities), sitting up and gathering the covers around me, chilled despite the muggy air. I'll do everything I can. Please, I said, grabbing a pen and paper and squinting as I turned on the light. I'm sorry, but I'm going to have to ask some questions. Is that all right?

Her exhausted voice shook, but she gave me all the details of Lia's accident. That the car had rolled on the highway and hit a tree, that Lia had been crushed but not killed, that in the hospital they'd operated. That Lia had died anyway.

Do you know where they operated? I asked.

This was University Hospital, Mrs. Stefanini said. Sorry, Elena. I should have mentioned it. That's why I called you. Will that make it difficult?

No, that's okay, I said, glossing over it, my stomach growing heavier, as if I'd swallowed cement.

Her breathing sounded liquid now, as she imagined her daughter under the bright operating room lights, the surgeons opening her up, and I remembered that she was a big crime show fan, meaning that her mental movie would be graphic. Such a small thing, really, the bits of your life you never expect to add up to anything, but now it would loom large in her mind.

Where were her injuries?

Her chest, she said. Why would that matter?

It might not, I said, thinking, *body parts,* not wanting to go down that road but unable to stop myself from recalling the tissue recoverers, the screeners and the processors and distributors, the medical company reps and the implant surgeons I'd worked among for years. To a large but mostly secret world beyond your family and friends, once you stopped breathing, your body was a resource. That was good, really; it helped a lot of people—a walk through the burn or transplant wards was all you needed to be convinced of that—but it could go horribly wrong. Had, with Mr. Stefanini, and often did, on my end of the spectrum. If, to the public, organ donation was a Hallmark-card moment, tissue harvesting was more like adult bookstores, big business no one wanted to discuss because they fulfilled a need barely acknowledged to exist.

I said none of that. Instead, I stood and began to walk and said, The more I know, the better. It should help me focus my search. Was there an autopsy?

No. Not that I know of.

That's good, I said, heading down the warm narrow hallway. My reflection in the window startled me, peering back in while I tried to see out; I turned away from the apparition on the dark glass and hurried on.

Is it good? Mrs. Stefanini said. No autopsy?

Yes, it is, I said, knowing that an autopsied, unclaimed body was almost always cannibalized for parts. I said, Did you sign any consent forms, for transplants?

I didn't sign anything.

Okay. That's a good thing too.

No, it isn't.

I'm sorry? I said, stopping in the kitchen, where the mismatched clocks on the microwave and stove blinked. Another round of thunder storms, another power outage, which I must have slept through, the second time in a week;

summer in Kentucky. Was Lia's death somehow tied to that? There was so much I didn't know.

Mrs. Stefanini said, I mean, I didn't sign anything because I didn't know she was even in the hospital. The accident was a few days ago. I'm sorry if this is confusing. It's still confusing to me.

Of course it is, I said. The wood floor was gritty under my bare feet. I wiped my soles on my unshaven calves and said, Don't worry. Take your time.

No, she said, growing angry, as if I was being willfully stupid. I don't mean confusing *that* way. I mean the accident and its aftermath are a mess. A complete, fucking, unadulterated mess. There was no purse in the car, and the car wasn't hers, and they didn't even have her name.

She was a Jane Doe?

No, Elena, not a Jane Doe, Mrs. Stefanini said, her voice cracking, the fight going out of her. When she spoke again it was nearly a whisper. They had her down as Cindy.

Paper rustled in the background and she said, Cindy Lownes.

Was she talking when she came in? Did she give them that name?

No, her boyfriend did. Belmont. Belmont Pitkin. Do you know him?

I gripped the counter so tightly my fingertips turned white. No, I lied, and immediately regretted it. What if she found out? Well, she couldn't have any lower an opinion of me than she already did. Still, it wasn't a good sign that in a crucial moment lying came so easily to me. I wanted to stop.

Was he in the car with her?

Lia took his car. Or at least we think she did. It's confusing. She'd been living with him and they broke up and it seems Lia went back to get some of her things and borrowed the car. For a bit, I'd lost touch with her. Her life grew . . . complicated. But he seems to have thought it was a new girlfriend, who he'd just had a fight with, this *Cindy*, so when the police called him about it, that's the name he gave them.

Didn't he go see her in the hospital?

They're both blond, evidently, both very tall.

But surely, I started to say, and didn't stop quickly enough.

Her voice quavering, Mrs. Stefanini said, It seems her face was battered.

Or, I thought, *he was drunk*. I headed back into the bedroom, eyes straight ahead so I wouldn't see my ghostly self passing again in the window.

I'm sorry, I said, disoriented and at a loss, and really, what else could I say? The words around death are never quite right and never enough, as they don't bring back the dead or erase the pain; it's like trying to fill a canyon one pebble at a time. Still, we have to try. And when did they clear it up? I said. This confusion?

After.

Okay, I said. So they had to switch around the names, and maybe something happened then.

Probably, she said. All of his girlfriends looked the same, I think. He gave them three or four names. She might have been listed under any of them.

The police know, I take it?

Yes. They're looking for her.

Good. That's good.

Is it? she said. Will they find her?

I lied again, knowing it was the right thing to do, even as I felt bad doing so. Her voice was so full of desperate hope that I didn't want to disappoint her. They should, I said, though truthfully a missing body wouldn't be a high priority. There hadn't been a crime, other than the stolen car, and the one who stole it was dead, so there wouldn't be any charges.

Can you help them? she said, meaning, *Can you help me?*

Of course, I said. Though they might not want me to. It would help if you let the detective know I was going to ask some questions. The police don't like to be surprised, I said, meaning, *The police don't like me.*

Yes, she said. I'll call him today. Or tomorrow, if you need some time.

No, I said, sitting on the bed again, though only the edge. I felt it would be somehow disloyal to move any deeper into it. I'm going down there now, I said.

Now? It's two thirty. You should sleep.

I felt a laugh bubbling up, that she'd called and woken me and now was worried about my sleep, yet thankfully I stifled it. Nerves, but it would have been hard to explain, and I doubted she'd be willing to give me the benefit of the doubt. How much pain could you cause one family before you started to despise yourself? I'd passed that point long ago.

It's okay, I said. I don't want more time to go by. It's been two days already?

Three, she said.

Not good, I thought, as that's usually the outer limit of how long anyone will hold on to a body. Okay, I said. I'll just shower and dress and get started.

She didn't respond and I thought maybe she'd simply hung up, which would have made sense, given all the horrible worries she must have had about her daughter's body, and that was the first time it really hit me that Lia was dead. I'd heard her say it, of course, but I'd just been startled awake and hadn't really processed it, and now as I did, I felt battered and stunned, as if a friend had struck me in the face with a brick as I went to hug her. I bent forward until my forehead touched my warm, bare knees and started to cry. Lia. My oldest friend. It must have been the sound of my crying that made Mrs. Stefanini go on.

Elena, she said, her voice thickening. I think she missed you these last years.

Then she did hang up, and I was incredibly grateful for her words, the kindness and the small measure of forgiveness they held, a gift of gold. I sat in the dark holding the silent phone, thinking that it's not often you get to try and balance the scales. They'd never be fully balanced—I couldn't wipe away the past, and some crimes are simply unforgivable— but even a small weight on my side was something.

Lia, gone. *Not possible,* I thought again, just a horrible mistake. We were supposed to reconcile. I'd let it go too long, though it had never seemed like that, and really, I knew that if it were ever to happen, the impetus would have had to come from her. On my bureau was a picture of the two of us at eighteen on the beach at Destin, the hill-billy Riviera, where half of Kentucky seemed to spend summer vacation or spring break. We were tanned and smiling, our legs buried in the sand and our brown arms raised as we held our mint juleps toward the sun. For the three years of silence between us, I'd never been able to put it away; some day we'd be friends again, I'd been sure of it.

Now I turned the picture face down on the bed and dug my nails into my palms so hard it hurt, not wanting to fall apart; I had things to do.

The image of her in a car rolling over on the highway came to me. The sound of it, of four thousand pounds of metal slamming into the concrete, over and over, throwing off bits of plastic and metal and glass, the tremendous bang as it hit the tree followed by a silence scooped from disaster, broken only by the hiss of escaping steam and ticking, cooling metal, of other cars screeching to stops. A 9-1-1 call, people rushing to the car, an ambulance setting out, its siren blaring. Too late.

She would already have been dying. Her heart had probably killed her, a half-pound weight crashing around in her body as the car rolled, still rocketing forward as her body recoiled from the blow of the air bag, tearing the delicately crucial aorta it hung suspended from like a precious red fruit. In dozens of autopsies I'd seen exactly that. That which gives you life also takes it.

I rocked on the edge of the bed, the cat up and rubbing against my legs, until the dial tone sounded, when I put the phone down and picked up the cat.

This is a good thing, I said to him. But of course it wasn't, since Lia was dead, and I burst into tears and buried my face in his warm dark fur, sobbing. He squirmed away, scratching my arm in his haste to escape, a deep scratch from which blood welled instantly. I sucked on it to make it stop, the coppery taste filling my mouth, and thought of Lia, of Mrs. Stefanini and her last words.

Elena, I think she missed you these last years. When I replayed them in my head this time, they no longer seemed to carry the tincture of forgiveness. Instead, beginning to imagine Lia's disordered life, I wondered if they weren't meant to apportion blame.

2

It was four AM before I got to University Hospital, a time I used to arrive there often. Tissue recovery happens at the oddest hours, and it seemed that whenever I was on call it happened in the middle of the night. A trick of memory, yet it still felt as if I'd been thrust back into my old life, and I had to stop myself from checking for my tools, the scalpels and skin shavers, the retractors and drills, which I'd always kept sterilized and ready to go during the ten years I worked for a tissue-recovery company, CGI. And, as in those times, I'd pressed frozen cucumber gel packs to my eyes before leaving the house, to reduce the puffy swelling, though this time, unusually, I'd left my phone at home. I didn't want any data about where I was going showing up in front of curious eyes.

But everything seemed now as it once was, that I'd returned to serving as a guide for the newly dead as they began their journey into the other world, the underworld, a kind of life in death, which had confused and exhilarated me—the exhausting work of mining the dead for the living. Oh, it was physical work I did, bones not easy to cut or break but necessary to harvest for those whose own bones had been eaten away by cancer or shattered in accidents or ruined by genetics, the gross motor skills called for there, and then the fine ones right after, stripping veins or tendons, ferreting out the tiny malleus and the tinier stapes bones, removing clavicles and pelvises and invaluable heart valves, harvesting collagen and corneas.

I remembered that during my years as a body broker, peaches lost their savor, that weather reports became a predictor of accidental deaths, ice storms especially, but even heavy rains were good, tornadoes like diamond mines surfacing on their own, whole families wiped out, the surviving relatives, distant and stunned, willing to sign anything, that the eleven o'clock news told me whether or not the next day might be busy, that death had its seasons: winter's murders, spring's suicides, summer's drownings, autumn's coal-mine explosions, that eventually I became a kind of weird human spider, hiding in my lair, waiting for yet another fool to wander into the sticky web of death. That I didn't fully realize it until the scandal broke, detailing my various misdeeds, thereby ending my connection with the Stefaninis, and turning me into a villain of almost cartoonish proportions.

* * *

I don't do well without breakfast, so I'd eaten a big one—eggs and Canadian bacon—despite what was ahead of me, and cleaned the kitchen (I've always hated coming home to a messy house, unlike Lia, who never let it bother her), and showered and stared at myself in the mirror for a long time before dressing. I was putting it off, afraid of violating my probation and filled with superstitious dread that once I walked out the front door I would make Lia's death real, and at last I knelt on the floor and prayed.

Not that I'm a believer, but I do pray at times, for strength. We live by hope, after all. But we cannot die that way. So I prayed for the strength to bring Lia home.

There on my knees with my eyes closed, I called up pictures of her: at the beach in her apricot bikini; at junior prom in a high-necked emerald dress that I'd been envious of and that had always been her favorite; of her smiling at me over her shoulder in front of a tobacco barn in Anderson County, the clumps of drying ochre leaves hanging down behind her in a long tunnel inside the black, slatted barn, every other slat thrown open for circulation. Whenever I looked at that picture, I could always smell those leaves hanging from the rafters, their seductively rich, ruddy scent, which was funny, since neither of us smoked, but we both loved the barns, the crop, part of our adopted heritage. It was what first drew us together in middle school, our shared outsider status—she was from Wisconsin and I from upstate New York—and then our mutual love of the landscape of the new home that neither of us ever felt quite part of. That was the picture I still had of her on my phone, though she'd stopped taking my calls and texts years ago.

The images allowed me to recall her loud, breathy voice and her loud footsteps too; you always knew when Lia was on the march, tall and so blonde her hair glowed at dusk. I hoped her death had left a similar kind of marking, would be remembered by those whose hands she'd passed through as she began her voyage in the wilderness of death. Otherwise I might not be able to do anything for Mrs. Stefanini, who only wanted to say good-bye to her daughter. Which I wanted too. Our quests would be the same, then, though our journeys would be different.

* * *

Broadway was deserted, the broad arcing pavement a pale fish-gray under the streetlights, no one filling up at the two lighted gas stations or spilling out of the three neon-signed clubs clustered on a single block, though the cop car lurking at the intersection of Clay turned my stomach.

I tapped the brakes and said, *Please please please*, hoping he wouldn't stop me. I no longer had a curfew as part of my probation—that had ended after eighteen months—but at this hour I'd still have a hard time explaining what I was doing in that part of town; bars were off-limits and there were all-night gas stations in my neighborhood and I couldn't tell them I was going to the morgue. Even a speeding ticket would provoke a potentially disastrous probation review. For nearly three years I'd been on probation; in another three months I'd be done with it and could go or work wherever I wanted, but until that time, a single mistake would likely land me in prison to serve out my sentence.

Yet the cop didn't budge and all the stoplights turned green for me, as if the city's transportation department had been alerted I was on my way, which wasn't a good thing. The closer I got to the hospital, the more nervous I became, and on Jackson, two ambulances idling at the dock, I felt as if I was going to hyperventilate, so I pulled over and parked. Prison, if someone reported me having been in the morgue; my PO, Joan, had been explicit about that from the start. The late hour would only compound my offense. But I wouldn't get caught, I told myself; I'd be careful. Not that I believed it.

I knew everything that was ahead of me, the sights, the smells, the sounds, the dim buzzing fluorescent lights of the overheated basement corridors, bleach, formaldehyde, the greasy scent of Chinese take-out, bones and bodies laid out for autopsies and anatomy students, the world I'd inhabited for fifteen years. Still inhabited, in a way, since I now worked in the Danville coroner's office, though not nearly in the way I once had. Only a part-time participant, an observer, mostly, whereas before I'd been a full-time body wrangler.

But I had to hurry. Odds were, seventy-two hours into it, that Lia might no longer be in the city, or that, if she was, she'd already been cut into constituent parts, depending on market demands. A swarming world descended on the dead, as coldly efficient as an army of beetles, and an unclaimed body in a hospital was like a zebra corpse on the veld. Everyone wants a part of it, and humans are the best scavengers of all: we make use of even the bones. Her skin would be shaved off and sold to burn units; her eyes plucked out for the corneas or for ophthalmological research or to harvest collagen; her shoulders, arms, torso, and legs used to practice new surgical techniques or refine old ones. Or her bones could have been removed, ground up, and mixed with polyurethane and metallic salts and cow parts to create implants for the living, jaws for facial reconstruction, hip, elbow, and knee replacements, discs for spinal patients, new molars to take the place of vanished ones. The list was practically endless. Useful, necessary, life-altering, but just as often a mark of vanity: new skin to cover newly enlarged breasts or old tattoos, collagen to plump thinning lips, fat to fatten tiny buttocks, pectoral implants for men, bone to sculpt a more pleasing jawline, and cartilage to turn up the end of a woman's formerly beaked nose. And all of it incredibly lucrative.

In the right hands, properly cut up and parceled out judiciously, Lia's body could bring back a couple hundred thousand dollars, after which what was left of her would be cremated, likely with several other donors, and finding her then would be impossible. I hoped it hadn't happened, hoped instead for the best-case scenario, that because she hadn't been autopsied she was still intact and had been shipped to one of the poorer medical schools, one without a willed-body program, which were always hungry for corpses. I knew, because for ten years, I'd tracked them down for those very schools.

At last I took a series of deep breaths and bucked myself up, since putting this off wasn't going to make it go away. *Nothing to it but to do it*, I heard Lia say, followed by her big, bubbling laugh, loud as a gobbling turkey. It was our eighth-grade gym teacher's pet phrase, which we'd adopted mockingly, but which had become a talisman, the way so much of life seems to accumulate around odd, unanticipated snags—God knows I'd never expected to become a corpse wrangler. So, with Lia's voice in my ears, I stepped out into the muggy, still air and made my way toward the hospital, asking a janitor outside on a smoke break to let me in.

You gotta go in the front, she said, pointing the way with her glowing cigarette. They don't want nobody coming in this way.

Her round, pale face was free of any makeup and partially hidden behind huge glasses and a tight helmet of blonde curls, and she seemed both tired and wary. She smelled of smoke and something spicy—Dr Pepper, I realized, when I saw the can beside her on top of a wheeled trash can—and was too young to remember me. Too bad, as I'd hoped some of the older janitors might be around. One of them might be more inclined to let me in, but then again, many had lost their jobs in the aftermath of the scandal. One more thing to feel bad about. Which I did, and which I used to my advantage, letting grief and guilt thicken my voice.

No, I said. It's okay. I'm going to the morgue.

Oh, she said, her shoe rasping as she scraped it over the cement loading dock, putting out her cigarette, a trail of sparks flaring behind her shoe like a comet's tail. Sorry for your loss, she said, and looked as though she meant it.

Thanks, I said, and touched her arm before she could go on. I don't want to have to go through all the paperwork just to get to see my dad, I said. I just got into town, and I know it's not the normal thing, but please, could you let me in this way? I used to work here so I know where I'm going.

When she didn't answer, I let my eyes fill up and squeezed her forearm, though playing her made my skin feel dirty. *Hush*, I told myself, *at least it's in the service of a good cause*. And when she turned to see if we were in line with the cameras (we weren't, I'd already checked) I knew I had her.

The old skills. To get at the dead, you have to know how to dance with the living.

She punched in the entry code, and I was inside a hospital again for the first time in three years, the first hallway brightly lit and smelling of the bagged garbage waiting to be hauled to the dumpsters, the next ones dimmer and with exposed pipes and whooshing fans and seven or eight narrow painted lines on the cement floor, each a different color leading to a different area of the hospital, and the next hallway with only one line left, the black one, dimmer still and descending and smelling of chemicals. Bleach and Pine-Sol and, faintly, but growing stronger, formaldehyde. As always, it reminded me of the scent of a vet's office. The air grew hotter the farther I descended.

She walked with me to the first turning, then watched me make the next one to be sure I really did know where I was going, and as I felt myself getting closer, my skin goose-bumped and the hair on my forearms stood up, an involuntary response. I'd always loved anatomy and autopsies, which was why I'd been so good, why I still was, and which I'd tried to explain to Lia a few times, unsuccessfully. To various boyfriends too over the years, with as little luck.

Most people don't want to draw back the curtain between this world and the next. But there was something about the human body that fascinated me, which was partially why I'd worked five years as a diener in this very hospital, and another ten as a corpse wrangler. Once again in recognizable territory, the quiet hum of distant hospital machinery a comfortingly soothing background noise, the uncomfortable subbasement heat both unwelcome and familiar, I began to whistle.

* * *

Outside the morgue, posted on a large metal placard, was a set of rules. No SMOKING, EATING, DRINKING, OR PHOTOGRAPHS IN THE MORGUE. DO NOT PLAY MUSIC—USE HEADPHONES. And, in larger, darker letters:

ABSOLUTELY NO ANATOMICAL MATERIAL MAY BE TAKEN FROM THE MORGUE WITHOUT SPECIFIC WRITTEN PERMISSION, AT ANY TIME UNDER ANY CIRCUMSTANCES. RESPECT THE DEAD.

They weren't new rules, but they'd never been posted when I'd worked there, and they were probably posted now because of me. I'd never been disrespectful, had never taken photos of myself with the newly dead or nicknamed the cadavers (*Beef Jerky* had been a favorite, though *The Admiral* wasn't far behind, given all the naval tattoos we saw), and I wasn't much for music, but of course I'd seen all of that, and more. It all looked bad, especially in the reports that came out, made sensational for the news, and a lot of it was—there was no positive way to spin the photo of a morgue attendant using a cadaver's penis pump to give the corpse a stiffie—but a lot of it had to do with a different way of teaching. Medical students and morgue workers, we'd all been brought up old school, which meant a certain callousness toward the dead, as a way to get past normal squeamishness. It wasn't easy slicing open an abdomen or cracking ribs to get at the lungs or cutting the skin of the forehead to fold back a face, and for a long time, the best way to go from this side of the curtain to the other was to make the leap with some disdain.

Now, though, anatomy courses focused on more reverential treatment of the dead, or most did, and that seemed to have taken hold here; everything was in order when I came in, though the years of underfunding had taken an obvious toll: the light still dim and unflattering (missing bulbs, flickering fluorescents), old machinery and ancient tools, dull, dented surgical stands, cabinet doors that wouldn't close or lacked handles, poor ventilation, and an autoclave that wheezed rather than hummed and that seemed to have been recently repaired by a blind man with access only to clothes hangers and electrical tape. A single attendant stood with his back to me at one of the tables, his bobbing brown head bent over some specimen.

A foot, which looked recently harvested, the skin still pink and taut.

Headphones on, he was partway through a dissection, repeating aloud a memory aid, so engrossed in his work that he didn't notice me until I was right beside him, at which point he looked up and pulled his headphones from his ears and said hello. Late twenties and tired; probably a med student. Behind him, on another table, a donated body was in the process of being embalmed. That there was only one body made sense; summer was always a slower time in morgues, and for some unknown reason, donations peaked in winter.

The corpse lay on a metal table, shaved and washed, a centrifuge pumping pink embalming fluid into the carotid artery through a long narrow tube, the tube taped to the neck so the pressure wouldn't blow it out. The right side of the body was already noticeably pinker, the skin beginning to blister. About half of the requisite three gallons had already been pumped in, but the veins of the hand were bulging, a bad sign, as it meant the fluid was being injected at too high a pressure and the attendant not paying attention; he should have been massaging the body throughout the process, pushing the blood out, allowing the embalming solution to flow in, otherwise the eyes might pop and the body become impossible to work on later. I didn't waste time pointing that out, simply lowered the volume on the centrifuge and opened the jugular drain tube to release the fluids, which jetted out at first, then settled to a more steady burble as they made their way down the channel cut into the table.

His glance went to my chest, not to check me out, but in search of a name tag, because of his inattention and because a skeletal specimen was next to the foot he was working on, which wasn't allowed. No doubt at four AM he hadn't expected anyone else in the lab, and if I was someone important—a doctor, say—he might catch hell for his double fouls: lack of care for a corpse and placing the specimen too close to flesh.

A nonexistent name tag didn't really tell him anything, but that I knew my way around the embalming process did; he slid a muslin sheet over the bones and smiled at me and said hello again.

Hi, Amed, I said, reading his name tag. Elena. Didn't mean to startle you. You look like you were caught stealing candy, I said, taking advantage of his discomfort. Without a word I picked up the injector gun from the corpse's stomach and lay it where it belonged with the other tools on a different tray; his third strike. *Respect, respect, respect,* I thought, knowing he'd had it drilled into him. Always treat the corpse with respect and be aware that family members might walk in at any point, which meant, among other things, not leaving tools on the body. Of course all of us had listened to the same sort of lecture and taken it to heart and then forgotten all about it as we became inured to death, or overwhelmed by work.

No, he said, and flushed quickly. It's just that I wasn't expecting anyone.

Sure, I said. Odd time. I let that hang a minute, and then gave him an out. That a recent amputation?

He smiled, unable to help himself. Yes. I was just trying to figure something out. There's a structure I've seen twice now in anatomy lab, and I wanted to look at it on my own. With his scalpel he pulled back one of the muscles and peered inside.

Hard to, when you're sharing with your tablemates, I said. Let me guess. Motorcycle accident?

Yes. He smiled again, impressed. How'd you know?

It's the same in most trauma centers, I said, not wanting to give too much away. He'd no doubt heard about the scandal, which had started local and quickly gone national: Reddit, Twitter, even CNN; if you Googled me it's all that came up. Besides, it was better that he be off balance. The less he knew, the more likely it was that I could get what I wanted. So I slid the muslin sheet back and picked up the specimen. Blood on the navicular bone. Without saying anything, I sponged it off and dried it and put it back on the central table, where it was supposed to be handled.

So, I said. You down here often?

Once or twice a week. He swallowed. It helps me pick up stuff that I don't get in the labs. I want to get better.

You're going to, I said. I'll bet you're the only one in your class who's doing this, right? Just try to keep things in their proper place, I said, and patted the specimen. It's important.

I know, he said, and nodded. His words started to tumble out. It's just that I got caught up in it and the foot stuff is so complex and I don't know. I mean, I do, I shouldn't have, but it just sort of . . . happened.

That's okay, I said. But I have to ask, you've heard about what happened here a few years ago?

He looked horrified and his glance flashed to the cadaver being embalmed, the veins of which were no longer bulging. The embalming fluid was moving smoothly now through the corpse, steadily pinking it. The selling of body parts? he said. I didn't have anything to do with that. I wasn't even in school then. Well, I was in school, but not anatomy classes.

Of course not, I said. It's not then that I'm worried about.

It took a moment for him to understand what I was saying, and during the lag the voice on his iPhone droned on, *Posterior tibial vein, tibial nerve*, and then the air conditioning kicked in and the rush of air seemed to make things click for him.

No, wait, you've got it all wrong, he said. He put down the scalpel as if holding it might somehow indict him and stepped away from the table. I'm not selling anything here. I'm *studying*. It's all science, I swear.

I'm sure, I said, and touched his forearm. Just like the janitor, he needed reassurance. It would be pretty hard to sell body parts out of here now, I'll bet.

I wouldn't know.

No, I didn't think you would. I squeezed, letting him know I was on his side. I complimented him on the job he'd done washing the cadaver, on inserting the eye caps and making the mouth look natural, on moisturizing the lips and eyelids, then decided it was time to get to my point before he either relaxed or became belligerently defensive. But what about the bodies? I said. Whole cadavers? Do you see them coming and going when you're here?

Well, he paused, looked at the table, turned the scalpel over, and aligned it with the Metzenbaum scissors. Sure, but I mean, they come and go all the time. People who die, the autopsies, the funeral home workers who come and get them.

And the willed bodies, the ones donated to our med school? The surplus ones we sell to other schools?

I don't know anything about those.

Not even where they're kept? You must know that. Orientation?

Sure. He was more animated now, happier, having something to tell me and suspecting that I wasn't going to worry about his minor infractions.

They're in room B437, he said.

And who's in charge of them these days, Dr. Handler still?

Yes.

Good. Thanks for your help. I'm going to look at them. The code still 3377?

4451, he said, and then, realizing what he'd done, Wait. That's supposed to be confidential.

It's all right, I said, pausing at the double doors. I'm not going to turn you in, Amed, for that *or* for mishandling the specimen *or* for minor cadaver mistreatment. Then I pushed through before he could say anything else, as it was better to get in the last word and leave him doubting.

Still, I didn't want to linger; he might develop a con-
science and alert a guard, though I suspected he still had no
idea who I was, and that I knew a former code told him I
had to be someone important.

* * *

Three-quarters of the storage drawers were full, some of
the bodies already embalmed, theatrically pink or tan or
brown or black, features set, eyes neither popped nor sagging, all looking younger than they would have at the time
of death, healthier too—embalming did that, smoothing out
their skin, plumping their lips—and I opened each one only
long enough to determine that it didn't contain Lia, always
a possibility since cadavers were sometimes mismarked.
But no luck this time; not one of them held a female under
the age of sixty. Not especially unusual—mortality rates
weren't high for that age group, and summertime had fewer fatalities. But still, something to contemplate. Perhaps
there'd been a run on young female cadavers for some new
surgical procedure; I hoped not.

Most of the bodies were ravaged, even after the embalming process.

The less, Dr. Giorgio had once called them, when, at
eighteen, I first began working in the morgue, having taken
the job as a diener on a dare. I must have looked appalled,
because he'd quickly added, Homeless, toothless, money-
less, friendless. Which means we have to take *more* care
of them, and here was proof of Dr. Giorgio's words, the

destitute and the drug addled and deranged, who came to the ER only as a last result and often too late, and who had no one to watch out for them after they died, no one to protect them, when their bodies became both useful and easily taken advantage of. To people like me, and by people like me, their body parts harvested and sold, often for good purposes and just as often for high profit; the violent second life of bodies, which nearly everyone was oblivious to and even those in the know refused to talk about openly. All the more reason Lia would have been valuable.

Finished, no wiser than when I'd begun, I washed up and headed up the long sloping hallway into cooling air, avoiding Amed, avoiding everyone, mourning that I'd missed Lia, and still with the foolish hope that she might somehow return. It all led to a nauseating swirling in my stomach, always, for me, a prelude to déjà vu. And just like that I remembered standing to the side of a third-floor operating room a decade earlier, just after I'd become a corpse wrangler, where a surgeon had kept his students behind to work on a woman who'd died on the table, wanting them to observe some technique. Ten minutes he'd held them there, fifteen, twenty, lecturing long after the woman's death had been recorded and now and then opening the abdominal incision to make his point more vividly, when, without any medical intervention on his part, the monitors had picked up a pulse. The Lazarus syndrome, he'd said, as shocked as I was to see her come back to life, and I realized what I'd been hoping: that mistakenly pronounced dead, Lia had somehow miraculously returned to life.

Oh, wouldn't that be lovely, I thought, knowing that I had a special affinity for the Lazarus woman because I'd been stillborn myself, or so my mother had been fond of telling me. She'd gone into labor in a bus station and only women were around and they all helped her, but even so I came out blue and still.

It was only the encircling crying women who seemed to bring you back, she always said.

Why only women? I'd always asked.

I don't know, she'd reply. Some kind of conference. Nuns, mostly.

Later, she said, Maybe it was fated from birth. You getting mixed up with the dead.

I don't believe in fate, I said, fingers crossed behind my back.

I don't either, she said, looking at me over her rimless glasses, but I don't know how else to explain it.

Now, I thought, if I couldn't live by the hope that Lia was secretly alive, I had to live by a new one: that I could find her. I couldn't restore her to life, but I could protect her body and accompany her to the grave.

I pushed open the loading dock door without a backward glance and lighted a cigarette and stood smoking in the humid air. Even here in the city the katydids and cicadas sent up their mechanical racket. The sky was just beginning to pale, though it was cloudy and smelled like rain. August in Louisville; seventy-five before dawn and a hundred before noon, water from the faucet warm enough to make tea, the air thickening and the massing clouds darkening into the inevitable ozone-scented evening thunderstorms: burnt toast and car exhaust and the hint of cooler air. But that relief was a dozen hours away.

A few more cars were on the roads, some delivery trucks chugging by, a handful of sleepy, silent pedestrians; the world was waking up. Not me, I thought, and tossed aside the cigarette and headed back toward my car, sweating after the stale air-conditioning of the hallways. If I felt eviscerated by Lia's death and uncertain about my chances of finding her, if I was out of whack with the world, having spent half my night chasing a body before others had even begun their days, I felt myself in familiar territory as well, returning to the one thing I'd ever been skillful at, a thing the world alternately despised and needed.

For three years I'd been despised. It felt appallingly good to once again be needed.

3

I wiped down the embalming table with a sponge first, so nothing splattered, then bleached it and hosed it off, and all the loosened epidermis and coagulated embalming fluid sluiced down the drain, leaving the nicked and dented table shiny and ready for the next body. I poured the drain and tissue buckets into the proper biohazard trash cans, sealed them, swapped the used scalpel blade out with the Qlicksmart remover and slipped it into the sharps container, then snapped off and discarded my latex gloves. Since I'd already slid the body with the McDonald's tattoo back in the cooler, I was done.

Done with the easy part, anyway. On the ninety-minute drive to Danville, past rolling hills planted with tall green corn and stubby yellow-green tobacco, past church after church after church interspersed with distilleries, past horse farms marked by miles of black running-board fences and cattle farms where Black Angus and bone-white cows clustered by the water troughs in the blazing sun, I'd thought incessantly about Lia and how desperate I was to find her. I had plenty of time, the drive slower than normal because farmers were going to their fields on their tractors and I was stuck in a long line of pickups behind them. We had Lia's name; we didn't have her corpse. And of course that made me think of McDonald's, a corpse we had in Danville without a name. She was well preserved, if a bit dry after five months in the cooler—no amount of Biostat could change that—yet we still had no idea who she was. McDonald's was about my age, about Lia's, and my boss Buddy had said after we'd had her for about a month that she could be my sister.

Gross, Buddy, I'd said. That's awful.

I don't mean it that way, he said, but you sure you don't have a missing long-lost relative? Same height, same hair, same facial features, mostly. And with your mother gone, you're both orphans now. Unlike you, though, maybe she was a woods colt. He'd had to explain to me that that was Kentucky slang for illegitimate.

I stood a crate next to the chute window and tilted my head up, breathed deeply, forcing the rank chemical scent from my nostrils. Car wheels, pavement, a dog lifting its leg. Such was the daily view from our belowground lair in the Danville coroner's office, which was in even worse shape than the morgue at University Hospital. At least that had been updated in the past fifty years.

When I closed my eyes, I saw the body of McDonald's again, mostly her right breast with the McDonald's logo tattooed across it, her singular identifying mark, the M of the golden arches curling around her nipple (tiny and light, so no children), the remaining smaller letters marching down her ample breast toward her sternum. An unusual tattoo, though it hadn't helped identify her. She was a Jane Doe, pitched in a drainage ditch off Route 127, the back of her head crushed. No sexual assault but all her clothes gone, all her ID too, so aside from the tattoo we had nothing.

Twenty-five, Buddy had said the day of her autopsy, before we'd opened her up to check her cranial plates, twenty-eight tops, while I guessed closer to midthirties.

Buddy had tapped a pencil against his lower teeth, mulling. You think? he said and straightened, hands pressed to his sore lower back. Why?

Her skin. I pointed to the darkened blotches of forgotten sunburns on the upper slopes of her breasts, then the smaller dark spots on her lip and forehead.

Those sunburns too? he asked.

Probably estrogen fluctuations, I said. They start around thirty.

He'd glanced at my forehead, visible above my mask, and I'd had to resist the urge to shake my bangs free.

All right, he'd said, penciling in thirty-five. You win again. Before I even had the chance to think it, he said, Like always.

Which was why he was a good coroner; he listened and learned. I liked those moments, teaching Buddy, the rare moments of communion we had, working on a body. And, of course, sometimes he taught me.

But that was about as far as we got with McDonald's. No missing woman was known to have a McDonald's tattoo, and dental records drew a blank. She had immaculate fingernails, no bruises or needle tracks, was tanned and ridiculously fit, so she hadn't been homeless. Her liver was free of hepatitis and cirrhosis so she hadn't been an alcoholic, and her organs were drug free. All of that meant that she wasn't a suicide or an accidental death, so we'd classified her as a homicide, and all of *that* should have meant that someone, somewhere, was missing her. But no one had come forward, and if they didn't soon, we'd run out of time; by law, we weren't allowed to keep the body beyond six months—even with a homicide—and we were at five-plus now. She would be the first body we'd have had to dispose of ourselves, and I guessed Buddy didn't want to have to deal with body brokers. Who could blame him?

Missing Lia, frustrated, I'd taken McDonald's out again, thinking we might have skipped over something important, but nothing was there, nothing at all except the tattoo, which had made me think of Lia, the twin fleurs-de-lis we'd had inked on the undersides of opposite wrists the day we'd turned eighteen. In celebration, but also false bravado, growing out of our foolish disappointment when both our breasts turned out to be too large for champagne coupes, which we'd read on a women's blog was the perfect size. If we weren't perfect, we decided, we could at least be distinctive.

* * *

From the open chute window an ambulance beeped as it slipped into reverse, meaning another body was on its way, and I made sure nothing was obstructing the slide. Sometimes the maintenance engineers leaned giant rolls of paper against it or piled up sawhorses, thinking it funny to make a mess for us since, like most old morgues, Danville's was in a subbasement—so bodies wouldn't putrefy—a holdover from the time before air conditioning. With the elevator out, ambulance drivers used the coal chute to save their backs, dropping them down without warning. Sometimes in the morning when I opened the office, if there'd been an accident on one of the parkways, I'd find bodies stacked on top of one another like pickup sticks. As long as the bodies were in body bags, bored drivers treated them like toys.

The body slithered down the chute in its black bag, and as I was wrestling it to the dolly, Buddy came down the long hallway from Maintenance, singing, off-key as always. That meant he was angry, which made me clumsy, and I nearly dropped the bag. Just before the door swung open I wedged my shoulder under the body and flipped it back onto the chute.

Wait, Buddy said. He stopped by the long row of nails sticking out from the wall at head height and pulled down his white lab coat. Both of us had cut our heads on the nails and learned to avoid them.

It's all right, I said, sweating, my gloves slippery. I got it.

I wanted to show I was trying, I always wanted to, since I was lucky to have any job at all, luckier still not be in prison. To get probation I'd had to have a job, yet getting a job was nearly impossible in the aftermath of being fired as a corpse wrangler from CGI, given the case's publicity; restaurants I'd once waitressed for wouldn't hire me as a dishwasher. Yet Buddy had hired me with few questions, which had been a double blessing; because it was a job, and because working in a morgue was one of the only things I was good at.

Now he shrugged his coat on and said, No, I'm not worried about that guy, and he began spooling and un-spooling his purple yo-yo. We've got something else.

He slapped a file down on his desk, and I realized he wasn't angry with me, which allowed me to breathe out.

McDonald's, he said. I see you already had her out. Weird. He flipped to a picture of McDonald's with paper bags over her hands, held in place by rubber bands, the way bodies usually arrived at a morgue. Suicide, he said. Or an accident.

Not possible, I said.

Oh really? His left eyebrow, the white one, rose. Why?

Because no one who took so much care of herself commits suicide.

He stopped spinning the yo-yo and I realized what he was thinking: no way he could use that as scientific evidence, even if he knew I was right.

Why is this coming up now? I asked.

The mayor's term is nearly up. He has to start running for office again in a couple of weeks. If she's a homicide, the murder rate rose on his watch.

Why do you care? If he loses, let the new mayor deal with it.

Harold loses, he writes letters to his successor, with recommendations whether or not my assistant should be retained. He'll get to me by cutting you.

I ignored my buzzing phone. Damn, I said, meaning, *I can't lose my job.*

Exactly, Buddy said. And McDonald's is the only case that can be reclassified.

What about this one? I rested my hand on the black bag's cool plastic zipper.

Car accident. Only question is whether he had a heart attack first.

I thought, *If McDonald's turns accident or suicide, cops won't search out her family.* They wanted to solve a murder, even a distant one. Changing her designation for the sake of covering the mayor's ass would be like killing her twice.

You didn't find anything? Buddy asked. Just now, when you had her out? The yo-yo spun from his palm to the floor and back in a purple blur.

No, I said, shaking my head. Not a thing.

Well, we'll look through other files from this year, he said and caught the yo-yo and pocketed it. His sudden stillness seemed like a type of noise and Buddy seemed to notice it too; his hand went into his baggy pocket to retrieve the yo-yo, and I held my breath, thinking he might cut himself. Besides his yo-yos Buddy kept food in there and a pocketknife and sometimes an uncapped scalpel, but his hand emerged unscathed, gripping a different yo-yo: mint green with a banana-yellow rim.

I don't have much hope about those other files, Buddy said, walking the dog with the yo-yo, studying its progress across the floor. People with the back of their heads blown off, a man stabbed fifty-three times by his wife. I don't see how we could change any of those.

Beside McDonald's file was an issue of *Mortuary Gazette*. Buddy picked it up and waved it, saying, I read in here how down in New Orleans they found a man with his hands bound behind him and two gunshot wounds to the back of his skull, and they still called it a suicide. But you know what? He tossed the journal aside, making McDonald's file flop open; her, during her autopsy. He closed it. We don't live in Louisiana. And I don't want to end up the subject of some expose.

* * *

That was a great fear, and one I understood all too well, having been the subject of one myself. Yet it hadn't deterred me from being hired, had perhaps even spurred it. I'd been dealing with bodies for fifteen years when Buddy beat out his only challenger for the job of Danville coroner, a female doctor, the sheriff's cousin. Buddy, Danville born and bred, had easily beaten the outsider. And I'd been out of work for three weeks when he started the job.

Buddy was a popular realtor before his election— everyone in town knew him—and he still kept up with real estate at work; the MLS site on the computer, flyers about open houses, etc. On really slow days he'd have me watch the place while he went out to show houses. He'd run for the coroner's job on a bet, he told me, had been surprised by winning, and had returned from his week-long training course, required of all non-MD coroners by the state, to one of the worst cases I'd ever seen, Danville's biggest disaster in decades. Nothing in his lectures and quizzes had prepared him for it, he told me over the phone, and he hoped to God that I could help him out.

An illegal fireworks factory had blown up downtown, destroying six buildings and killing nine people. Windows shattered five miles away. The day I interviewed was the morning before the explosion; I'd left thinking I didn't have a chance, but the next morning he called me at seven AM. If I could get to work within two hours, I had a job. I was there in seventy-five minutes.

We recovered one hand two miles from the blast, still in its yellow work glove and holding a manila envelope, though we never did locate the arm that went with it. Limbs and torsos had been blown everywhere, one headless body cut clean in half, blue intestines curling from the gaping hole, while two blackened heads rested in a bush, face to face as if they were kissing. Buddy threw up twice at the site, several more times back at the morgue.

The sheriff, still angry about his sister losing, had made things miserable for Buddy—*A fucking realtor as coroner,* he said—but I'd helped Buddy through it, instructing him to see the body parts as puzzle clues, as impersonal as the bags of gunpowder. Wires from a chest meant a pacemaker, metal rods in a leg indicated surgery. We started piecing people together from their medical histories and, when the sheriff ragged us for taking so long, I told him it wouldn't ever have happened if he'd been doing his job: the factory had been in a boarded-up building five blocks from city hall. He backed off and bit by bit we stitched the bodies back together as best we could, nine bodies from thirty-seven body parts, having to guess on only a few.

Nothing else was ever as gruesome, not the occasional floaters from the Kentucky River, not the decomposing old folks who'd baked when their AC cut out during heat waves and the electrical outages that followed thunderstorms, ripening as no one had checked on them for days, and after we were all done Buddy repaid me by never once indicating he thought less of me for what I'd been involved in. Once, though, after reading a newspaper report about yet another budget cut for the coroner's office, he'd asked me how the body parts market worked. I'd filled him in, but the next day he'd told me to forget he asked, and I had, though I'd never been able to forgive myself for having polluted him. My work as a diener at University Hospital had introduced me to the trade, and, after college—where my communications degree hadn't produced any job offers—I realized body brokering was more lucrative, and, as simple as that, I'd disappeared down the rabbit hole. Part of me was probably wishing Buddy would do the same thing—the guilt of others might lessen my own—but most of me was glad he hadn't.

* * *

All morning after his announcement about McDonald's, I went about my chores quietly, chafing at what we were being asked to do, vexed that I couldn't get away to track down Lia. Lunch, I told myself. At lunch I'd ask Buddy for the afternoon off, and in the meantime I kept quiet, helping Buddy as I could.

He worked on the new guy without speaking, a bad sign, and leaving off the music of Arvo Pärt, a worse one. Every time he played him, it meant Buddy was happy.

I took photos of the corpse fully clothed, and then photos of him nude and unwashed. Before we washed him and took the last set of whole-body photos, Buddy turned on country music, music that made him angry, so I knew he'd made up his mind: McDonald's was going to be reclassified. The music was a kind of scourge, to punish himself for caving.

Putting the bodies back together years before had been hard, awful work over long days and longer nights, and the toll on Buddy had been ferocious. Bags grew under his once luminous brown eyes, filled with fluid, grew darker, turned blue and then black, as if they'd been tattooed, as if they were paved. They'd never disappeared and he seemed to have aged a decade a day. But if it was shocking, it was also why I had a job now and why I knew what was coming, my stomach growing heavier throughout the morning, filling with clay at the thought of it, with dread. I was going to be the one to reclassify McDonald's.

It would be his signature on the report—it had to be, to be official—but I'd do the actual typing, about which he was superstitious. If you wrote it, it was yours, the actions, the meanings, the morals. He'd been protective of McDonald's from the start, and one night, still going over the files as I left, he sat bent over the desk, not looking up from paperwork so white in the pool of light it glowed. As I reached the door, he said, When my sister died, she was around this age. We never found out why.

For all of his loquaciousness it was one of the few personal things he'd ever told me, though it took me a moment to realize it. So I would type in the changes, hating to do it to McDonald's but telling myself that of course she'd never know. I wouldn't be hurting her, not in a way that would matter to her, at least, and I'd be doing it for Buddy and, more selfishly, for me. Who knew when having him owe me again would come in handy?

I wanted to slice my palm with a scalpel for thinking that way, but I knew that wouldn't stop me. Finding Lia was too important to allow time for nobler sentiments. After all, I'd been the one who put all those things in motion years before, my fault, my fault, my fault, something I believed and told myself so often it had become my mantra, something I hummed in the shower or while chopping vegetables for yet another homemade soup—I didn't go out much anymore—or sitting bored at a stoplight, waiting for it to change. And often, peculiarly, the chanting was in Lia's voice.

* * *

Buddy rallied when checking the new body for distinguishing marks. Vietnam, he said, running his hands over the man's puckered left thigh. His wallet had revealed him to be a veteran, but it was the scars Buddy was looking at, glossy, raspberry-colored, wrinkled indentations on both thighs, trailing down the left shin like an archipelago.

Land mine. Exactly how I got my scar, Buddy said, referring to his thigh. I'd seen it only once, when he came directly from a pool party to collect and autopsy a cadaver found in the woods.

It was May, and we'd driven out to Dreaming Creek to fetch the body. Buddy had told me to bring water. As we made our way down through the wooded hills toward the burbling creek on an old game trace and I started coughing, I knew why: a strong wind moving through the leaves with a sound like rain, blowing a mist of lime-green pollen from the trees, which clogged my nose and throat.

Sycamore and oak, Buddy said, waiting in the dappled light as I drank. They like creek beds.

I tried to talk but my throat was too sore, so I took in the landscape instead, the thickly treed hills dotted with pink and white dogwoods still blossoming though the canopy overhead had begun to leaf in, the rarer but more spectacular redbuds, with their masses of black raspberry–colored blooms, and the creamy white magnolia flowers, as big as owls. If you were going to die, I thought, it was a beautiful spot to do it.

A dozen people clustered by the creek. I wanted to push ahead because they might be contaminating a crime scene, but Buddy held me back with an extended arm.

Wait, he said. No crime. It's a drowning. That's why there's no police.

How do you know that? I croaked.

They told me.

They? The men were in brown short-sleeve shirts buttoned to the neck, the women in long, simple burgundy dresses. They looked like few people we ever saw in Danville; maybe the Mennonite honey sellers who set up occasional Saturday farmers' markets in a deserted bank parking lot.

Kin, Buddy said. When I looked at him he shrugged and said, Distant. The only kind I have left. That's how I knew to come.

A woman knelt beside the drowned man, who'd been dragged from the clear shallow water and lay face down on the muddy bank. Two men stood in the creek, on limestone slabs so smooth they looked placed, and the woman was holding a baby with a port-wine stain covering half its face. She took the dead man's hand and touched it to the birthmark.

Okay, Buddy said, dropping his arm. He's ours now.

What was that about? I asked.

They think it'll make the birthmark disappear. He's the baby's father.

Before attending to the body, Buddy shook everyone's hands, even the women's, so I did the same. The men helped us bag and carry out the corpse, but even so it was getting dark as we turned to make our way back up the hills, which seemed twice as steep now, twice as slippery; the men carrying the body had to stop every ten yards to let Buddy and me catch up. The women went ahead through the trees with flashlights, singing through the dusk, something that surprised me by sounding celebratory. A psalm, I guessed; I was too shy to ask which one. The nesting cardinals in the darkening trees began to sing and whistle too, as if in response, with their clear, piercing calls: what cheer, what cheer, what cheer, wheat wheat wheat.

Now, Buddy said, if anyone tries to take out those leg bones, they'd better be careful.

I knew what he meant; the metal splinters could cut badly. Had, many times, on careless bone removers, myself included the first time I'd come across one, a WWII vet. All kinds of things got blown into legs in accidents and times of war; with road rash you always looked for gravel, but with war injuries the subsequent gifts were mysteries. Watch sprockets and gears or a bit of a photograph, a Gillette razor blade, the name still clearly written after fifty years, on one vet three embedded molars, as if some enemy had bitten down on him in his final agony. But Buddy fell quiet after discussing this guy's wounds, though he did crank the country music up to deafening levels when he began handing me the internal organs to weigh.

At eleven—the Episcopal church bells sounding through our open window—Buddy finished the last bit of sewing on the heart attack, snipped the thread, and tossed the needle in the biohazard bin. The king is dead, long live the king, he said, the way he ended all autopsies and obituaries. I'd always meant to ask him where his little Britishisms came from, but now didn't seem the time.

He peeled off his gloves and said, About McDonald's, she had no defensive wounds.

So it's an accident, right? I said.

He opened her file, noticed a chunk of concrete in a picture. That could be blood, right? He laid his finger on a dark stain covering one corner. Could be what she fell back against. Maybe it was that weird lunch she had.

He'd commented on her stomach contents during her autopsy—pomegranate and pears. Now he said, Maybe she was dizzy from lack of protein.

A chunk of concrete four feet from her body; how could she have fallen against that, Buddy? But I already knew she was going to be an accident. Okay, I said. I'll make the switch, after I clean up here.

Good, he said. I'm going to take an early lunch. Make sure you send an amended report out to all the police departments we initially contacted, telling them they no longer have to worry about a murderer on the loose.

Buddy? I said, before he left the room. Can I have the afternoon off?

His shoulders stiffened, but I wasn't worried he'd say no. I'd heard him talking to my PO earlier in the morning, as he did daily, confirming I was at work, and though she could drop in at any point unannounced, she wasn't likely to drive the ninety miles from Louisville to Danville. Who could blame her? She'd gone to the University of Louisville, and the only flags that outnumbered the blue University of Kentucky's on the drive down were Confederate ones, both of which infuriated her. But even if she did, Buddy could say I was running errands for the morgue, which would be enough to keep me from violating my probation and ending up in prison. Or so I hoped.

It's something personal, I said. Something important. I couldn't tell him what because the PO often asked if I was breaking any rules: dealing with corpse wranglers; marketing tendons or heart valves; contacting medical researchers; visiting morgues or funeral parlors. And I knew Buddy: if I told him the truth, he'd feel obligated to pass it on. *Promises aren't piecrusts*, he'd once said. *They're not meant to be broken.*

He seemed to understand that and nodded again, rubbing the lemon-scented disinfectant into his hands. Don't do anything stupid, he said, and pointed at me with glistening fingers, which made me shiver.

Too late, I thought. But I said, No, of course I won't. I've already done enough stupid things to last a lifetime. And Buddy, I said, just as he reached the door. Keep McDonald's around for a bit, okay? Now that we're going to reclassify her, maybe something unexpected will come up. It always happens that way.

He held up two fingers, which for a bizarre moment I thought was a victory sign. Then he said, We've only got two weeks, but I will. His eyes glistened, though I only realized it when he wiped one with his shirtsleeve.

He said, I'd keep her forever, if we could. Until we knew.

I realized then that he had the sickness, this attachment to the dead. For me it had been sheer numbers that did away with it, body after body after body, so that they blurred together into a river of death and I became merely another set of hands they passed through on their way to their final, distant shores. That wouldn't happen here, couldn't; Danville simply wasn't big enough. It wasn't all bad—a reverence for the dead was something I'd parted with too easily, and in McDonald's case I was beginning to feel some of the same things as Buddy—yet it could lead someone to concentrate on the dead at the expense of the living. And once that happened, there seemed almost no way to come back.

* * *

After he left, I searched through McDonald's file one more time, stopping at the details of all the women she might have been—their names, their birthdates and Social Security numbers, a bit of their family histories. In my worst moments, when the scandal seemed like it would never end, I'd wished that I could die and come back as one of them, or take one of their identities and move on. Once I'd said as much to Buddy.

You couldn't, he'd said. Wouldn't be right.

I know, I said. It's not something I'd actually *do*. Just something I wish I could. And really, it's not that I wished I were dead. Just that I could have a clean slate. Without that, it seems like I'm always going to be running from my past.

That's not what I meant, he said. It's not that you need to suffer for your sins, but that sooner or later someone might find you out. You'd use their Social Security number to get a job, and a cop or a PI would track you down because the parents were still hoping you were alive. It would hurt them, you know?

I could always use Carmine, I said. And in truth, I'd had a fake ID made up for myself in that name, just in case.

He gave a bitter smile. Sure.

Carmine Semple was an orphan and a missing person, but no one was really looking for her. Her name had come to us from the Georgia state police when we were first trying to uncover McDonald's identity; she'd gone missing from an Atlanta waitressing job and from her still-furnished apartment, and the Georgia police hoped we might solve their case, one they left open but didn't seem to find particularly troubling. Because Carmine Semple was known to have a peculiar tattoo (though exactly of *what* was unknown), when we learned of her, Buddy hoped we'd finally found our woman, that he could at last give McDonald's some closure. Even if she had no family, she could have a name, a burial, a headstone. But no luck, since dental records and DNA from Carmine didn't match with McDonald's, no luck, and now we were going to make it worse by reclassifying McDonald's as an accidental death—yet another discarded dead woman, left to fend for herself in the next world as she probably had done in this one.

I amended her report on both the computer and the page, as Buddy had asked, reclassifying her death as accidental, wrote a group e-mail to local and regional police departments explaining our reasoning, and sat for a good ten minutes deciding whether or not to hit Send. A train whistled mournfully outside of town, a car honked nearby, crickets chorused in the heat. Finally, I couldn't do it. This was the first time I'd ever gone against Buddy's wishes, but I felt so dirty reclassifying her in the morgue that I couldn't bring myself to send her changed status out into the world. *It's all right,* I told myself, deleting the email and shutting off the computer. *There'll be time enough for that in the weeks to come.*

It was absurd and wrong and irrational, yet before I put McDonald's file away, feeling that something had changed, that now that we'd rechristened her as a newly minted accidental death long after we'd swapped her blood for formaldehyde, now that her paperwork would be filed away and forgotten, I wanted some tangible link to her past. So I took out the sheet with the names and vital information for all the women she could have been, should have been, and folded it into squares and stuffed it in my purse. Finally, as old-timers in the country around here sometimes did, I picked the shiniest quarter from the change clustered in the bottom of the bag and tucked it under McDonald's tongue.

It was supposed to bring luck to the dead, and lord knows McDonald's needed it. If I weren't so superstitious, I'd have tucked one in my mouth too.

4

I was back in Louisville, back near University Hospital, just after lunchtime. It had stormed as I drove, the drumming, sheeting rain so straight up and down it looked ruled, cars pulled to the side of the road or stopped in their lanes to wait out the sudden blackness, so dark it felt like an eclipse. Twice I'd come close to rear-ending one of the parked cars, a Midwestern phenomena that drove me crazy, and then the sun had come out and the cars sped up, surrounded by individual clouds of mist as if they were all smoking, ready to burst into flame. I'd run by my apartment just long enough to grab my old files from under the kitchen counter: *Doctor Sold Cadavers; Body Brokers Gone Wild; Dawn and Dusk for the Dead*. In each of the articles the Stefaninis had sent me—dozens—my name was circled in red.

Now the air was dry and cool, a rare, pleasant break for August in Louisville, when the temperature rarely dropped below ninety, and on impulse I decided to kill the remaining two hours over an outdoor lunch, glad I'd brought a sweater. I was anxious to see Dr. Handler, but she taught late-afternoon and early-evening hospital practicums and didn't show up until at least three, and sitting outside her office for two hours seemed foolish. People were sure to remember me. The Garage was an old gas station converted to a pizza and shellfish restaurant, its parking spots a freshly graveled seating area, its bays a bar.

I wasn't the only one attracted by the weather, so I had to wait for a table, which didn't bother me, as it allowed me to flip through the files while I sat in the shade under the plane trees lining the sidewalk, half of their leaves already spent, an autumnal bell-pepper yellow after enduring the long summer heat. If anyone had asked why I'd brought the files, I wasn't sure. Perhaps to remind myself that I'd started out one way and been surprised to find myself another? Hardly original, but still, my fall shamed me, and the articles laid bare all my sins in merciless detail.

How I'd left my position as diener at University Hospital to go to work for CGI as a corpse wrangler; how five years into it a friend's father died and I'd harvested his skin and collagen, his heart valves and patellas, his femoral fascia and cranial bone and spine without permission; how I didn't tell his family for another five years and wouldn't have ever, if a reporter hadn't informed me of an upcoming exposé about illegal body brokering featuring me as the central character; how this was all part of my system of illegally recovering body parts from Louisville-area funeral homes, working with funeral directors when they knew, with funeral parlor employees after hours when they didn't; how I recovered the same body parts from area morgues, operating rooms, and ERs, working with corrupt nurses, doctors, and surgeons; how I created false identities to sign permission slips for tissue recovery when permission hadn't been granted; how I falsified the ages of corpses and causes of death so tissue processors received body parts from us that came only from patients under fifty who were free of cancer, hepatitis, and AIDS; how even when I had permission to remove certain tissue from bodies at area hospitals, working in those cases with good doctors, nurses, and surgeons, I'd taken extra parts to sell on my own; how I created false demand for surplus cadavers from the willed-body programs at the University of Louisville and the University of Kentucky, saying that I was transporting them to smaller medical schools in desperate need of corpses and stripping them instead; how a venal funeral parlor director worked with me, combining the various cadaver parts left over after stripping—corneas and ligaments and heart valves from one body, a spine and tibias from another, hips and collagen from a third—and cremating them together, then parceling out the cremains into various bags so that each package returned to individual families weighed roughly the correct amount; how immensely profitable this had been for CGI; how willfully, perhaps criminally blind many of the hospitals and clinics and big surgical suppliers I worked with were to this entire dirty business.

What wasn't in the articles was that I hadn't known it was Mr. Stefanini when I was stripping him—his face covered with a bag, as corpses often were, his name already falsified on the papers—or how after harvesting Mr. Stefanini and realizing my mistake, I hadn't told his family because I knew it would cause them more pain; how in the five years after that there seemed no way out other than to keep harvesting cadavers, to do it again and again and again to stranger after stranger, whether or not I had permission to do so, telling myself that it was a good thing I was doing, that burn and accident victims, that the genetically unlucky or accidentally wounded or intentionally self-destructive would profit from my profit; how I knew that truth to be both convenient and not quite the entire story even as I endlessly repeated it; how being brought up short when the fudged paperwork and loose accounting and complete lack of permissions for so many stripped corpses finally caught up with me came as a relief. Or how through each day of the last three years, even that sense of relief made me feel guilty, because there had always been an out and I'd never taken it, until I had no choice.

* * *

Eventually a table opened up and my eyebrow-pierced server came and introduced herself, though so quietly and with such diffidence that I had to ask her twice to repeat her name, and I ordered a salad of local greens and a plate of jambalaya in honor of Lia. On the drive in I'd played an old zydeco mix she'd made for me, trying, as always, to convert me. Though she'd been born in Wisconsin, her father's family was from Louisiana.

Just burn me a Jesse Colin Young CD, I'd asked her. He's handsome.

Those are old pictures, she'd said. *He's* old. And she'd burned the CD she wanted to. When had she not done things her own way? One of the many frustrating and admirable things about her.

I'd listened to a few songs before snapping it off, unable to take any more, which made me feel guilty, so the jambalaya was contrition. Foolish, I knew, but I couldn't stop myself, nor from wondering what McDonald's favorite music might have been, her favorite food. While I waited, I pulled my sweater more tightly around me against the chill and listened to two twentysomething men who looked like refugees from Brooklyn—bearded, suspendered, porkpie-hatted—discussing a new beer garden in a Louisville neighborhood rechristened NuLu a half dozen years earlier by the city council.

When the name change was first announced, Lia and I had argued about whether it was smart (because if you didn't try, the city would never change) or pitiful (an attempt to make Louisville seem like a hip city). We'd both been passionate, both argued our cases extensively, almost endlessly, but now, I couldn't remember which side either of us took. And when I called up her voice in my mind, I imagined her arguing both sides with equal conviction, which puzzled me. Was I losing her in the process of trying to find her body?

I'd asked for unsweetened iced tea, something that, before moving to the South, I'd had perhaps once a year and that I now drank almost daily, and I'd finished two glasses before a waiter refilled my glass for the third time and said, I could leave the pitcher here, if that would be easier.

Embarrassed, I looked up at him. Dark and handsome, but why was he wearing scrubs, and what had happened to the woman who said she was going to be taking care of me? Why was he staring at me as if I were a freak? Had I been talking to myself as I imagined Lia?

He smiled, holding the half-empty pitcher out as if I should take it.

Sorry, I said. The weather's made me thirsty.

He put down the pitcher, smile fading, and said, You don't recognize me?

I studied his face, and when I said, Amed! he smiled again.

Is this your job? I said. It would make sense; medical school was expensive.

He laughed. No. I'm taking a break and I saw you here.

But the pitcher, I said.

I know. He leaned closer. Don't tell anyone, please? I don't want to get thrown out for unauthorized borrowing.

He really did have a nice smile, dazzlingly white teeth, full lips, caramel skin, though in the sunlight I saw fine lines around his eyes. Thirty-ish then. Like me, though I'd been -*ish* now for several years.

All right, I said. Promise. Your secret's safe with me. Just don't do it often. Eventually they'll catch up with you.

He turned serious. I don't, he said. I never have. This is my first offense. Then he smiled again. Can I join you?

The question was so unexpected that I couldn't think of a suitable refusal, and in the long pause while I debated my reply, a gusty wind sprung up, bending the plane trees, and a cloud slid in front of the sun, casting Amed in shadow. At last I said sure and closed up the folder and put it on one of the seats, though not before his glance had swept across it.

Wanting to steer the conversation elsewhere, I asked if he came here often.

It's open late, he said, and after some shifts I like to have a drink on my way home. I live a few blocks that way.

Butchertown? I said. That's pretty. Or parts of it, away from the railheads and slaughterhouses. And it was, leafy and green, the oldest part of the city, filled with long, low one- and two-story wooden houses urban pioneers were beginning to gentrify. Ornate doorways, ornamental brick, Lia had called it a shelter mag's wet dream, but I knew it chiefly as great hunting grounds when I'd been a body wrangler.

An apartment in an old house from the late 1800s, Amed said. All new appliances. Across from a church complete with a steeple and bells.

Ah, so you were a realtor in another life, I said, thinking of Buddy.

He laughed again, and I liked how he gave his whole body to it. Lia had too.

I suppose so, he said. I'm leaving out the bad bits. The scent, whenever the slaughterhouses vent. If I didn't have air-conditioning, I couldn't live there.

The waitress introduced herself to Amed and took his order and I found myself with a curious sense of contentment, sitting outside in a city restaurant with someone else on a warming, sunny day. Nothing I'd expected when the day began.

As if he'd read my mind, Amed said, So you don't mind, really? That I foisted myself upon you?

Foisted? No. Not quite the proper verb, I said. Though you were forward.

He bowed his head in mock guilt.

I reached across the table and patted his hand. Don't worry, I said. If I'd really minded, I'd have had a ready excuse.

Oh? You get hit on often?

You sound surprised.

Ouch, he said. You're good at making me sound bad. I only meant that I'd be interested in hearing your standard rebuff.

No.

Okay, he said. The direct approach.

Wrong word again, I said. Direct *response* to a direct approach.

And if it doesn't work?

Then I pull out my medical knowledge. Say I have TB or the plague or throw out some term in Latin that sounds vaguely dangerous. *Ad partes dolentes.*

Don't know if that would work here, he said, glancing at the crowd, many of whom were also in scrubs, one woman holding a lime-green parasol against the sun. Too close to the hospitals, he said. Too many people who wouldn't fall for it.

True. But I don't often need it.

Hard to believe.

I shrugged, feeling pleased. I'm not in this part of town much these days.

His Coke came and he toasted me and drank it down, and I was surprised to find that I liked watching his throat, that I noticed his nice neck, strong without being thick. Surprised too that I'd been flirting with him. Unexpected, as was his sudden shift in the conversation.

So what are you doing over here now? he said, leaning forward. Something to do with those files? He nodded toward the chair.

Those? I said, disconcerted, feeling chilled. Those are old.

And yet you have them with you.

Yes, I said, and pulled my sweater more tightly around me. I decided to tell him just enough to satisfy his obvious curiosity. I'm going to see Dr. Handler later.

But Handler wasn't involved in that, right?

I felt myself flush. No, I said. That was the previous head of anatomy.

Dr. Giorgio. I know.

Then why are you asking?

Because you came by this morning and now you're here again and I wonder what ties it all together.

So that's why you sat down, I said, growing angry, though more at myself than at him. It was foolish to think that any conversation, however innocuous, could be unfreighted by my notorious past. To cover my embarrassment, I searched through my purse for my phone, a pen, a wand to wave and make him go away.

No, he said. It's why I first came over, I'll admit. But not why I sat down.

That disarmed me, slightly.

Listen, Elena, he said. I'm sorry. It's just, given everything, I wondered what was up. But you don't have to tell me.

You know about my past then?

Sure, I know about your past, he said, settling back and stretching an arm over the seat beside him. Hard not to, working at University Hospital. You're the cautionary tale we all get told. You're on parole, right?

Probation, not parole, I said. I never went to prison. *Though I might,* I thought, *if this goes south.* Yet that he'd said parole rather than probation reassured me; if he *had* researched me, he'd have known that many were unhappy with my probation, demanding prison time instead. Mrs. Stefanini most of all.

Still, I didn't like where this was going and sat forward, wanting to take charge again. But you should also know that I'm out of it, I said. No longer a proponent of career opportunities for cadavers.

Don't joke that way, he said.

Oh, please, I said, lowering my eyes as my face grew hot. We all do, it's how we get by in that business. Making fun of the cadavers and their products. It's too grim to contemplate otherwise.

No, that's not what I mean.

Then perhaps you should say what you do mean.

I meant, don't do that. As in, don't make a joke of it. That line, career opportunity for cadavers? That sounds practiced and protective, a way to distance yourself from what we do to one another, the living and the dead. Yes, I know all about the case, but I also know that behind it, beyond it, was something else. There had to be, right?

Oh, a mind reader, are you? I said, and sat back.

I'm just saying, nobody gets into this field for bad reasons, and nobody thinks it's going to make them rich. At least not at our level. The higher-ups, well, they're a different story.

It was a small gift, this reference to the rapaciousness of the surgical supply companies, which had been the focus of the suits springing out of the scandal but not of the news outlets that covered it, and I felt my anger cooling. It cooled more when the waitress came with our salads and I had a chance to collect myself.

After she left, I said, So did you know this morning?

Who you were? He picked up a forkful of salad and ate it and said, Yes, though not right away. His lips, which were very nice, were shiny now with oil. After you left I figured it out.

And now you want to figure out why I was there?

Yes, he said. I have no idea.

I told you, I said. I'm going to see Dr. Handler.

Right, he said, his glasses glittering as his head titled up. You're going to see the head of the willed-body program. That's fine. And maybe it has nothing to do with your previous problems. That's fine too. He leaned forward before going on. But if you're going to see her, why come to the morgue at four in the morning?

I hesitated, thinking that he might be able to help me—he worked in the very morgue Lia had gone missing from, after all—yet I wasn't sure I could trust him. What did I know of him, really? What was to stop him from telling the police I'd been there, or Dr. Handler, or anyone at University Hospital? Still, I might have said something if only to get him on my side, to insure that he kept my visit a secret, but our entrees came, the waitress crunching toward us over the gravel, and at the sight and scent of the jambalaya I thought of Lia. How she loved northern winters and despised Louisville summers, what a good cook she'd been—the things she could do with garlic and potatoes, crayfish and clams—her annoying habit of clearing her throat when she was about to criticize you. That made my eyes fill, and Amed reached out patted my shoulder, misunderstanding what had happened.

I'm sorry, Elena, he said. It's really none of my business what you're doing at the hospital. I didn't mean to upset you.

I found myself grateful for Amed's kindness, even as I felt guilty for taking advantage of it to shift the conversation to food. It felt so good to talk with an attentive listener about something other than death that, after I paid and got up to leave, I bent and kissed Amed on the cheek, startling both of us.

* * *

When I got back to my car, the driver's side-view mirror had been torn off and lay cracked and useless just beneath the left front wheel. Someone driving by too closely, I speculated, and picked it up, which was when I noticed the slashed rear tire and burst into a full sweat. Both rear tires had been slashed, it turned out, both mirrors torn off, and the front passenger door left unlatched. The car was a mess: the glove compartment thrown open, the central console. Bending in to restore a loose order to the CDs, the maps and manuals and receipts and old lipsticks scattered about, I found the rear seat torn up, yellow foam springing out, and the car filled with an atrocious smell, the foul remnant of a rotting skunk.

The art gallery I'd parked in front of was deserted, the nearby restaurants closed, and no pedestrians were walking by, but Muth's Candies was open and I went in, the old-fashioned bell over the door ringing behind me. I asked the two women behind the boxed chocolate stacked on the swaybacked wooden counter if they'd seen anything.

My lord, no, the larger one said, and pushed the back of her beehive hair up as if my asking the question had flattened it. Then the two came out with me to stare in the warming air at the damaged car.

Goodness, that's awful, the younger one said, her skin turning pinker. I can't believe we didn't hear anything. Wait here a minute, she said, and disappeared inside and came back out clutching a one-pound box of milk-chocolate turtles. As a gift, you know, she said, handing it over. To make you feel better.

And as we silently contemplated my damaged car, I found that the gift and the group made me feel unexpectedly less secure. If by myself it might just possibly have been some weird random event, in the company of others, equally surprised and upset—so upset that they needed to try and make it better—it came to seem more deeply personal. Inevitably, I wondered if this had anything to do with my pursuit of Lia. But who would do such a thing, and what was I supposed to learn from it? To be afraid? Of what? It made no sense, and because of that, it unsettled me all the more.

Honey, the older one said, seeming to intuit my thoughts and leaning her damp face within inches of mine. You made someone angry. You be careful now, you hear?

5

I was still out of sorts when I got to Dr. Handler's office, having walked to University Hospital through the growing warmth while the car was towed to a tire store. Dr. Handler's secretary remembered me.

Are you here for personal reasons? Mrs. Hopper asked, and from her tone, she might have called up my mug shot on her computer.

Business, I said, looking down at her.

Business? she repeated, unhappily. And do you have an appointment? She ran her pen down her calendar, open on the desk before her.

No. I was hoping to see her before her four o'clock practicum.

She doesn't like to be disturbed before the first session with the new med students. Probably best if you make an appointment for another day.

With the pen she flipped through pages of the appointment book. Already she was a week ahead.

Still the old-fashioned way? I said. Mrs. Hopper's one weakness had been talk, an aggrieved sense that people treated secretaries as, in her words, *in-and-outers*: you fed them facts and they passed them on, or they had facts and spit them out. This was especially true of doctors, and knowing that had for a decade allowed me access to invaluable information.

I thought everything was automated now.

It is, she said, and tapped the computer monitor with the pen. I'll put it in here after, but I'm old-fashioned.

I ignored the jab, but I couldn't completely hide my irritation, drumming my fingers on the half wall. Did that bring the smallest smile to Mrs. Hopper's face?

I'll just wait, I said.

But she's not free before class.

That's all right, I said. I can walk with her. All I'll need is five minutes. I'm sure she won't mind.

Which wasn't true, as Dr. Handler had told me several times that she grew terribly nervous before each semester, though she'd been teaching for years. Which Mrs. Hopper knew.

I just don't think that's a good idea, she said.

You could just announce me. See if she can make time now. If not, I don't mind waiting. I've got all afternoon.

Oh, all right, she said, and called.

No, she said, looking at the calendar again. Nothing before your practicum. She nodded and said, I will, yes. Thank you, doctor.

You may sit there, Ms. Kelly, Mrs. Hopper said, indicating three small chairs on the other side of her desk wall. Dr. Handler will see you shortly.

Thank you, Mrs. Hopper, I said, using her surname intentionally. Very kind of you. I know you're busy.

She glanced sharply at me, but, satisfied I wasn't being facetious, she softened. Well, I *do* try to do my job, she said.

Telling her she did it well would be laying it on a bit thick, so I took my seat and waited quietly. Around the walls were blown-up full-color photographs from Churchill Downs on Derby or Oaks, Louisville's annual golden moments. The Derby pictures were taken down the stretch, long views of bunched, sprinting horses, clods of dirt churning up behind them, or close-ups of the colorful jockeys, their crazy-quilt silks, or pans of the packed, boisterous grandstands. In one, dozens of spectators held drinks out toward the camera, their faces joyous and depraved, like devils sick of sin, Lia had once said, a line I was fairly sure was a quote. We'd made annual infield treks on Derby Day, fifteen dollars for a day-long bout of drinking and misbehavior, races on top of the port-a-potties, mudsliding contests when rains turned the turf to swamp, fewer and fewer clothes as the day went on. Once, Lia had given me her shirt when I'd become separated from bra and blouse just as the police began rounding up the nudes. It seemed that every year she'd looked out for me.

Those pictures, I called to Mrs. Hopper over the divider. Are they yours? Did you take them?

No, she said, her voice quiet. My son.

Oh, I didn't know he was a photographer, let alone such an accomplished one.

She didn't respond, which surprised me, until I remembered donating to a memorial fund in his honor. Awful that I'd forgotten, awful that the woes of others could be so swiftly cast aside, but others' troubles waned as our own waxed; only one moon could rule the sky, there could be distance between the living and the dead. Mrs. Hopper being Mrs. Hopper, she wouldn't say anything to me about it, as strangers weren't meant to be privy to private grief. Then I had a worse thought: What if his body had been mined for parts without permission?

There seemed nothing for it but to sit silently, and I did, focusing on a photo featuring a dozen women, primped and pampered looking, which reminded me of Lia. Not the look, but our reaction to it. Remember, she once said, the best way to think of Derby fever is that it's a kind of semi-permanent junior prom state. And she'd been right about that—a two-minute race that required half the city to lose its mind for a full month leading up to it.

I smiled and grew sad, missing her; how odd that Mrs. Hopper and I should both be in the midst of private grief, unable to comfort one another.

Ten minutes later Mrs. Hopper rose to get some letterhead from the supply closet, her face averted. I couldn't see her eyes, to gauge if she'd been crying. She was dressed in a matching blue skirt and jacket, their lines a bit dated, but wearing racy, expensive shoes. *Beautiful*, I thought, even as I knew I'd never wear them, not only because I didn't get out much but because I didn't have the legs to carry them off. The heels high and definitely not academic, the straps highlighting her glorious calves, hinting at a subterranean rebelliousness. I'd never have guessed. Surprises at every corner today.

* * *

My phone rang—Joan, my PO.

Not wanting Mrs. Hopper to overhear me, I stepped into the hallway.

In a clipped voice, Joan asked if I'd been associating with the wrong people.

What? I said, icy sweat breaking out under my arms. Of course not.

A phone call I just had says otherwise.

Amed? I wondered. But it couldn't be him; he wouldn't know her or her number. Who said so? I asked.

You know I won't tell you that, and that it doesn't matter. Where have you been? Let me guess, you're not at work.

No, I said, certain Buddy would have called if she'd called him. But perhaps, worried, *he'd* called her. Better to be honest. I'm at University Hospital.

Doing what?

Work. For Buddy, Mr. Alix. Something he needs to know about in Danville.

You're not in their morgue, are you?

God no. Never, I said, and crossed my fingers. It was as if she knew, the silence she made me endure.

Finally she said, Be here by five. You're going to take a drug test.

Joan, you haven't tested me in eighteen months, and I've never failed one.

So you'll have no problem passing this one. In fact, be here by 4:45. People like to go home.

All right, I will, I said. I've got a meeting soon so it might be close.

Her sigh sounded theatrical. Don't screw it up now, Kelly. In three months you'll be done. Three months out of three years. Get the damn test in on time.

* * *

I knew I'd pass, but I was spooked. Joan didn't give second chances and her suspicions had been raised. Who had called about me? The same person who trashed my car?

Worried that my voice had carried, I tried not to get rattled by Mrs. Hopper's disapproving frown when I returned, but luckily Marie was at last ready to see me.

I wasn't sure how to greet her—it had been four years, since weeks before the scandal broke—but she clasped my hand in both of hers and said, Elena, so good to see you! How've you been? Which eased things.

Fine. And you? Your perfume? I love it. Rose and jasmine, vanilla.

Good. I just switched, and I worried it was too much.

Not at all, I said. Sultry. What is it?

She laughed. Coco Noir.

You look wonderful, I said.

You think so? She touched her hair, the big copper cuff on her forearm catching the light.

Yes, I said, and meant it. The reassignment surgery had been quite successful, the chin more pointed, the nose smaller, the Adam's apple nearly invisible. Her forehead was beautifully feminine, smooth and flat, unbossed. That must have taken some time, given her former look. Her skin was exquisite—for a moment I imagined a blaring headline on a women's mag: *Bad Skin? Try Transgender!*—her lips lusciously plump. Collagen injections, no doubt; perhaps even from skin I'd shaved in all my years of work.

And work? I said. Head of anatomy now! Must not be easy.

She grimaced as she sat, gestured to another chair. We're making do. But making do means working with less and less. It's not easy.

I thought of the morgue's jury-rigged equipment, the amputated foot resting on a battered mayo stand, the wheezing, barely functioning cautery.

It must be tough, I said.

It is, she said, and sat back. And Mrs. Hopper tells me you wanted to see me about business. Is that so? Are you, she said, and paused, searching probably for the right way to say it. Getting back into the field?

No, I said.

Her relief was palpable, her shoulders and neck relaxing. My appearance was more troubling than I'd expected; she must have been wondering if she was going to have to refuse me something, perhaps a job. Not easy, because we'd been friendly if not exactly friends, coworkers during the five years I'd been a diener and she the head of the hospital morgue. Though she'd been male then.

What, then? she said.

Well, I said. It's just that a body has gone missing.

From the hospital? Her eyes widened in alarm. I'd have heard about that.

Probably not from here. But I wanted to check. I filled her in on Lia's accident, the mix-up about her identity, the disappearance of her body.

But I don't know anything about this. I'm not sure how I can help you.

I'm sure the hospital had nothing to do with it. I just wondered if the willed-body program had begun sending cadavers to other hospitals again.

She grimaced again, then stood and closed the door more tightly. I understood why. The program had been suspended in the scandal's wake, the program head fired. Marie had taken over, once it restarted, promising to make body donations 100 percent informed consent. No more indigents, no more unclaimed bodies from the ER, no more shipping donated bodies elsewhere. It hadn't happened.

Those state budget cuts, she said? They've hurt the hospital more than the university. Our department chair has asked us to raise money any way we can. So yes, some of our bodies still go . . . elsewhere.

And tissue donations?

She glanced down at her hands, clasped in her lap, spread

them apart and put them back together, looked up at me. We've set up a tissue recovery room, she said.

Not surprising, as there'd been talk of it while I was working, but not what I'd hoped to hear. A good cadaver—disease free, in relatively good health—would provide heart valves, muscle, tendons, and veins. Cranial bones, leg, arm and spinal bones, cartilage and ears. Skin, of course, twenty-two square feet per body, and collagen galore. The hospital would see little enough of the money generated by these—which couldn't be sold but came with enormous processing and handling fees—yet the room rental would return a hefty income.

You know, she said. We were against it at first, but the university has suffered through a dozen budget cuts in a dozen years, and upper administration kept pushing us to find ways to make money. This is about the only way the anatomy department can find. No rich donors hope to name a morgue.

I understood the pressure. I'd often felt it myself, though in different ways: to produce twenty cadavers a month, to harvest more skin than anyone else, to supply CGI with the necessary number of spines and corneas and pelvises each quarter. At times it had been overwhelming, and when not enough bodies came through the regular channels, I'd started haunting more and more funeral parlors and area morgues, discovering along the way which ones were willing to work with me. Once, drinking with Lia and spilling my anxiety, she'd said, You know, jobs that don't involve dead people are often less stressful.

Well, Marie said. I wanted to explain. I'd forgotten her habit of looking away during a conversation and then glancing back, of blinking her eyelids closed as she did. Now, facing me again with her eyes closed, it seemed as if she had to steel herself for what she was about to see upon opening them.

And have any been harvested recently? I said. The last few days?

Cadavers? More than likely. The trauma center. And this time of year there are always car accidents. Vacationers. I can get the information. Still, I doubt any of them would be your friend. You say the police are looking into this? They would have contacted me if the problem was on our end. But wait here, she said.

* * *

While she was gone, I examined Marie's pictures on her walls, happy to find myself in one taken fifteen years before, at a Lexington senior-citizen conference; prime recruiting ground. I was still a diener then, Marie still head of the university morgue, and we'd set up a booth among pharmaceutical reps and the elder-care homes and medical-device stores, with a simple sign: FREE BURIALS. I'd thought it too forward but Dr. Handler—Mark, in those days—said it would be like catnip.

The elderly are pretty unsqueamish, and many want to help, he'd said.

Shouldn't we make the sign about that then? I'd said, but he'd nixed the idea.

Still, I liked that he treated death with a sense of humor—not something you often ran into—a big part of the reason I'd gone with him.

And it had worked. Again and again, people stopped to ask what we were selling, what the catch was, and Mark or I would explain: The University of Louisville's medical school needed cadavers so its med students could learn anatomy and its surgeons could create or master new surgical techniques.

The last place they should try something new is on the living, Mark would say, and go on to extol surgical experimentation's virtues.

One silver-haired woman named Wilma, with small shoulders and an oversized head, asked what would happen if we got too many bodies.

Well, that would be a nice problem to have, Mark said.

Nice why?

Because if we didn't need the bodies for our students, we could give them to other medical schools that don't have enough—and believe me, there are never enough—and if we still had too many then, we could harvest tissues and eyes. There's a massive need for that kind of thing, and it has almost biblical effects.

Oh? she said. I knew you doctors were arrogant, but now you claim to bring the dead back to life?

Mark had an easy, voluble laugh, and when he loosed it then, several other passing seniors stopped to see why.

Well, he said, we're not gods, but the eyes will give us corneas, which means we can help restore sight to the blind, and the ligaments will repair ruined knees, which means that the lame can walk, and heart valves are even better. Especially for children.

Well, she said, I was hoping it would help me in the here and now.

It already has, Mark said. That knee, right? A new one. She had a large scar running down the front of it, peeking out beneath her long linen shorts.

A *fake* one, she said.

Yes. And I'm guessing it's a few weeks old from the way you're walking, which means that donors have helped you, even if you didn't know it. The first knees were implanted on donors, and the cement that keeps the new knee in place is made from a paste of ground-up human bone.

Really? she said. I didn't know.

Mark leaned forward and whispered loudly, Trade secrets. And it's not just knees that cadavers help with. Ever had an older friend's face go from a raisin back to a grape?

That made Wilma laugh and nod.

Well, a surgeon implanted fat. And guess where the fat came from?

From there, I handled the informational part. If Wilma agreed to donate her body upon death, we guaranteed that it would be used for medical purposes and that, within three years, she would be cremated and buried at no charge.

Buried where? she said. I don't want to be left in some abandoned field.

No, of course not, I said. The spot would be of your choosing.

Really? Wilma said, seeming doubtful.

Yes. It could be a family cemetery, or, if you don't have one, it will be in a specially reserved site in Louisville.

Wilma picked up a brochure and read through it. A few of the other conference-goers were watching her, awaiting her decision.

But I've been a University of Kentucky fan my entire life, she said. I'm not sure I could live with myself, ending up at the University of Louisville.

Mark, a recent transplant to Kentucky, was flustered into silence, but I understood the depth of the rivalry in a state with no professional sports teams. Almost no Louisville fans lived outside the city, though the city was peppered with Kentucky fans, and the local saying was that if a Louisville woman married a Kentucky man, it would always end badly. So I said to Wilma, That's all right. The good thing about our program is that you won't have to live with your decision.

It took a moment for the joke to register, but when it did, she tipped her head back and laughed, almost as loudly as Mark had.

All right, she said, and began filling out paperwork. Who'd have thought? Eighty-three, and for the first time in my whole life, a college has come to recruit me.

* * *

Upon her return, it took me a few startled seconds to adjust to Dr. Handler as Marie all over again, especially since she was even younger-looking than in her photos. If she noticed me studying her she didn't let on, though perhaps she was used to people being startled, and perhaps she'd become good at covering it up. Even as Mark, she'd been something of an actor, her mask slipping after that Lexington conference when we'd gone out for drinks and Mark had looked briefly melancholy.

All right, I'd said. What is it? We've just done really well—twenty-three new bodies in the pipeline—but you look disappointed.

Not disappointed, he said, swirling his scotch. Perhaps just . . . concerned. Sometimes I feel like I'm greedy for the dead. A bit unsettling, you know?

Now, as Marie, she said, These are the deaths we've had since last week, and the disposition of the corpses. Her voice had a peculiar hesitancy. The one you're talking about, Cindy Lownes? She was released to a funeral home.

Any tissue recovery? Or organ donation?

She flipped through the files. No, nothing marked. And it would have been. We have pretty strict controls now. *After the scandal,* she didn't say, but the words filled the room nonetheless, making it seem newly crowded, as if the shelves stuffed with medical texts, reference books, and bound journals had suddenly inched closer. She hurried past the moment. Released to the Hapsburg Funeral Home, on Monday.

Lia's mother hadn't known that, I said, jotting down the name.

Marie glanced out the window at the first yellow leaves

falling from a black walnut tree in a sudden wind and turned back to face me.

Sorry, she said, working the copper cuff up and down her forearm. I have a confession to make. She cleared her throat, and when she spoke again her voice had its old force back. We made a mistake.

A mistake? With her body?

No. She shook her head. Nothing like that. Paperwork. We had a student worker filling in. I only figured it out when I looked through everything. It's good you came, actually. Some of the paperwork was misfiled. *Her* paperwork was misfiled. That's why the woman's mother wouldn't have known.

Oh, I said. Well, that explains it.

Marie was silent for a few seconds—leaves ticking off her open window—but finally she said, May I ask you a favor? This would look bad, if it got out. After everything.

Of course, I said. How about this, we never had this conversation? There are a lot of ways I could have discovered it. I'd hate for anyone to get in trouble over a small mistake, and it's an enormous help to me.

She put her hand on mine across the desk in gratitude. Thank you. Do you know anyone at Hapsburg? Someone who could help you?

I did, or had, as it was once one of my recruitment spots. After I'd left U of L to become a full-time corpse wrangler for CGI, it was one of the places I'd had the most success at. I said nothing about that to Marie, just that I was familiar with the funeral home.

She puckered her lips as she scratched her head, a

gesture I remembered Mark making; odd, to see how little some things had changed when so much else had. It was like looking at one of those optical illusions, where at first you see a beautiful young woman with a hat, and then an ugly old woman with an enormous nose; Mark, Marie, Mark, Marie, the old him in the new her, one underlying the other. Like all of us, I suppose, only we're never forced to be so obvious about it.

I seem to remember that funeral parlor being involved in all that mess.

Yes, I said. I think the owner had to sell it.

Well, I hope the new owners aren't like the old ones. But even if they aren't, I don't know that it will matter.

Why not?

If they've got any of the same people working there, it'll probably be just like it always was. People don't really change much.

I didn't have anything to say to that, given all that she'd gone through to become Marie, given what it implied about me.

As if my silence indicated what I was thinking, Marie's face fell, and she gathered up her papers on her desk and started to apologize. Well, of course, she said, that's not exactly true, is it? I mean, some people can change a lot. Look at you!

Or you. But I didn't say that either; she'd meant no insult, and her change, though it had been in the works a long time—hormone therapy, facial hair removal—had been speeded up by the scandal, when she'd been forced to take a leave of absence while culprits at University Hospital were identified; she'd used the time to finally undergo gender-reassignment surgery. A benefit, really, as it allowed her to come back to work as a different person once she'd been cleared.

Still, the awkwardness was palpable, and we were left looking at one another until a church bell rang the hour, the peal of its pleasing bells drifting in through the window behind Marie, who turned to look outside at the sound, as if the bells would be passing by as they rang.

When they were done, Mrs. Hopper knocked on the office door. Dr. Handler? Time for your practicum.

Right, thanks, Marie said, and stood and grabbed her purse, a beautiful burnt umber affair with complicated straps and clasps. Nothing I'd have guessed Mark, or Marie, would carry.

Sorry, I said. I didn't leave you any time to prepare.

Oh, it's fine, she said, really. The less time I have to contemplate it the better. She gathered up a pink file and waved it. Lecture notes. Not a lot has changed about the body since I started teaching this course twenty years ago, so it's not like I don't know what I'm doing.

Still get nervous about it though? I asked.

Terrified. But I find that, after the first few minutes, once I can get someone to laugh, I'm okay. I just hope my jokes don't bomb. If they do, I'll be a mess for the entire hour.

We headed out into the crowded, noisy hall, shoulders bumping as we made our way against the surging students, most of whom seemed headed to downstairs lecture halls. So young-looking, it depressed me.

We turned sideways and they passed around us. When we came to a sort of clearing among them, Dr. Handler said, May I say something?

Of course.

You're too young for all those regrets. Her smile seemed a sad one. Do yourself a favor, and don't hold on to them.

Oh, I said, startled, unsure of how to respond.

It's just, she said, and breathed in, as if girding herself for an unpleasant task. I know about your probation. We all do. She lowered her voice. And I'd hate to see you do something to violate that.

Was this a friendly warning or a subtle threat? I felt instantly chilled, which must have shown on my face.

Oh, no, she said, coloring. Not that. I knew I'd say something stupid. It's just, you didn't always look out for yourself before. I want to make sure you do so now.

6

Outside, sweating in the renewed, smoky heat, I thought of calling Lia's mother or the detective whose name she'd given me, but the detective might say something about my probation—Marie's warning had not been in vain—and knowing where her daughter had first gone would only get Mrs. Stefanini's hopes up. Uselessly, perhaps. As I didn't think she could bear further disappointment, I followed the crowd toward Broadway, hoping to flag down a cab.

A shift change at the hospital; tired, quiet adults, tired, cranky children. One girl in a mint-green dress kept begging for Cracker Jack from a food cart; her obese, angry mother slapped her, but I said nothing because I knew nothing about her life. Her plastered-down hair, her disheveled clothes, maybe her own mother was dying, maybe this small act of violence was her grief leaking out.

An explanation, not an excuse. I'd seen all kinds of crazy things when asking people to sign donor protocols. One woman had agreed, then chased after me and torn up the paperwork, screaming that she'd recognize her son's eyes, while a man had once slammed me against a wall and accused me of being in league with ER docs in refusing to provide care for his grievously injured mother, having read about just such a scheme on the web. Once a distraught mother berated me and the transplant surgeon who'd waited only the requisite seventy-five seconds between her child's death and opening him up to harvest his heart and lungs, while siblings often came to blows over whether or not their parents would have wanted their bodies donated, even though paperwork clearly showed they had. I'd even had ambulance-chasing lawyers appear outside the operating room, shouting about parallels to the case of Colleen Burns, declared dead in a Syracuse hospital and waking up as the organ-recovery team's first scalpel slit her skin.

I sped up, in order to get as far away from the angry mother as possible, glad that Lia's body had been released whole. If she'd been harvested, restorative devices would've been tucked into her body—wooden dowels for long bones, pvc piping for the shorter ones, putty for eyes, false teeth for any missing ones, foam and body powder to fill space left by plundered organs—and she might already have been cremated. Ashes to ashes and ashes *with* ashes; donated bodies were often cremated en masse, though doing so was illegal. Of course, legality and corpses rarely mixed, and once you were gone, almost no one was there to protect you.

I knew the quicksilver routines of death. The wrangler called the nursing supervisor to schedule recovery (an odd word for it, as recovery had meant something entirely different hours before to hopeful relatives) and then the patient would be transported from the morgue to surgery once again, this time to be stripped down like a stolen car. In an hour, two at most, everything would be done: the bones and tendons and veins bagged and labeled, the skin soaking in a saline solution, the eyes and windpipe on ice, the drainage sluiced away and the work surfaces cleaned, the floor mopped, the instruments washed and decontaminated. The operating theater would look as if nothing had happened.

Someone else would undergo surgery in it soon, be taken apart and put back together and, if they didn't make it, return an hour or so later to be more fully disassembled, as if it was some kind of bizarre factory, even more studious about pulling someone apart than it was about putting them together. Very little was lost in the process, and much gained, or so we told prospective donors, and ourselves, and generally it was true. But with money involved, sometimes we weren't as careful as we should have been, or as respectful, or as honest. You can lie about bones.

My first supervisor at CGI had told me that, and getting into the pine-scented taxi now I heard Kevin's words again. Everyone needs bones, he'd said, but everyone wants them young. Few donors are over forty, and no donor has ever died of cancer.

Good, I'd said. No one wants bones riddled with cancer.

No, he said, his green eyes unnaturally large behind his square glasses. You don't understand. No one who's ever donated their bones has ever died of cancer.

It took me a few moments to understand that he meant their records were falsified.

Don't be shocked, Kevin said.

And I suppose I shouldn't have been; he'd been in the business forever. When he'd started, they were still using pigs at surgical conferences because pigs' anatomy was roughly analogous to humans' and because there were no corpse wranglers around to supply the necessary cadavers; he had funny stories of some of his improperly sedated potbellied charges escaping once in a Chicago Hilton.

Telling me about donors, he said, Whether we tinker with the facts or not, it's not as if it really matters. We sterilize the stuff so much, nothing that could harm anyone will ever get through that process.

But why? I said.

Simple. Ten thousand corpse donations a year nationwide, one million transplants in the same time frame. After blood, the thing we need most is bones, so look around and do the math. The perfectly healthy aren't in the habit of dying. What people don't know won't hurt them.

As the taxi sped off, I thought, *If only he'd been right*. Or rather, if only what people hadn't known had remained unknown, it would have been better for everyone. Yet even as I thought it, I knew it wasn't true.

* * *

I hated Joan's noisy, busy office, not because the criminals in various phases of their long, semiperpetual journey through the criminal justice system made me feel unwashed, but because there, I realized I belonged with them. *The less*, I thought, remembering Dr. Giorgio's phrase, as these were the people among whom, after death, I'd gathered most of my specimens, the very ones he'd tried to safeguard. Which of course now included me, less than whatever I'd been before.

There weren't many ways to become *the less* other than drugs and mental illness, so it was quite an accomplishment for me to have discovered a new one, but I was certain now that I was heading to prison, that there was nothing I could do to stop it, not if I wanted to find Lia. And I did. I did. I wanted to ease her mother's aching heart, and my own.

But Lia, I thought, *I'm so scared.*

No answer from her, though I'd wanted to be shown some way out, to be given one last chance to set things right, to take back all the inattentiveness and foolish choices that had brought me here, the trapped rabbit's final prayer before the patiently voracious fox. Yet the response of the universe was to turn my bones so cold they felt like they'd been stored in a freezer, to ice my skin as if I was already dead, a corpse waiting to be plundered.

Perhaps that *was* Lia, I thought, letting me know what it had been like for her at the end. And though it was the worst possible place to do so, I began to cry, quaking uncontrollably. Misinterpreting my mood, Joan required me to take a Level Two drug test. For the first time ever.

* * *

After passing the tests, I taxied yet again, this time to Michel's Tires to pick up my still-mirrorless and smelly car, and drove with the windows down and the air-conditioning blasting to the Hapsburg Funeral Home. The funeral director was busy with a client so I waited in a spacious anteroom, disoriented after coming in through the front door. I'd entered often enough through the back in my working days, though always at night, as funeral directors don't like to be bothered by tissue-recovery teams and complain constantly about their work: The removal of skin or bones or eyes compromises corpses, leading to leaking embalming fluid or faces difficult to make presentable.

As team leader I would turn left into the cooler to be sure the body matched the info we had; as a team member I turned right and prepped an embalming table, sterilizing it, draping it, laying out tools. Once the body was wheeled in I'd draw fluids for the serology report—hepatitis, HIV, septicemia, or syphilis meant we had a clunker—and during the court case I was forced to admit that only rarely did we reject a body. That we did reject skin (the body was too old, the skin too thin) never got reported, since it didn't fit with the gruesome storyline, and the press, like the rest of us, likes things neat and sharply shadowed. Gray areas cause trouble.

Two potted palms in brass urns stood inside the waiting room, as if this were an old-fashioned night club, and I sat beside one and leafed through a pile of *Sports Illustrated*s until a middle-aged blonde in a short banana-yellow dress came in, sobbing. She leaned her forehead against the far wall and began to shake, her shoulders, her legs, her entire body. I was embarrassed, suspecting that if she knew I was there *she'd* be embarrassed, so I let a magazine fall to the floor and fumbled with it, giving her time to recover.

What are you doing here? she said, as if I'd snuck up on her.

I'm sorry, I said, standing. I'm just waiting to speak to somcone.

Just as suddenly as her anger had flared, it winked out. Of course, she said. I'm sorry. It's just that everything happened so quickly.

Yes, I said. But please don't apologize. I can never decide whether someone going quickly or lingering is worse. Neither is ever very good.

No, I suppose you're right, she said. Though in this case I wish I'd had a chance to tell him what a bastard he was.

And with that she left. I was still turning it over when Mr. Hapsburg came in, a kindly older man whose handshake was neither unctuous nor crushing. Not wanting my name to ring a bell, I introduced myself as Carmine Semple—Buddy's orphan—and explained that I was there about the case of Lia Stefanini, who had been picked up by a Hapsburg driver. I added that the corpse was most likely listed as Cindy Lownes, as that's how University Hospital had her down. He escorted me through hushed underlit corridors to his office, where a portrait of Abraham Lincoln, the embalmers' hero, held pride of place behind his

ornately carved cherry desk. Lincoln had supported embalming, then a fringe and nascent art, to allow the return
of Union dead to their families; he'd also ordered his own
corpse embalmed upon his death. In the wake of his long
funeral train journey back to Illinois, during which millions
of Americans viewed the president's preserved corpse, embalmers went from outcasts to accepted, from accepted to
respected, and the business of the dead bloomed for them,
a vine with a million moneyed flowers. My career had been
an offshoot of that vine, and though in my case respect was
unlikely, I'd gladly take acceptance.

Sorry, he said. I don't remember the deceased, and I
need to check up on her.

The police haven't called? I asked.

They probably have. But I've been away for a couple
of weeks.

He was tan and I wondered where he'd gone, but it
didn't seem appropriate to ask, though I found myself wondering where a funeral director vacationed, then wondering
why a funeral director's vacation should seem so strange.
Everyone needed a break from work, those working with
the dead most of all; when they weren't out of town, funeral directors were on call twenty-four hours a day.

I remembered Kevin, my old CGI boss, prepping for his
vacation by writing down addresses of morgue attendants
we worked with.

For what? I'd asked him.

Postcards, Kevin said. *Wish you were here.* The personal
touch is important in our business.

He told me to try it and I had—once, from Cancun, where Lia and I had gone together—but it felt so creepy that I'd been unable to do it again. Kevin did, and always from Bermuda, where, I later learned, corpse plundering was both legal and thriving.

Yes, Mr. Hapsburg said now, glancing through an orange file. Cindy Lownes. She was here, briefly. Someone from the family came for her. They wanted to use another funeral home.

Mrs. Stefanini arranged this? I said, confused.

No. He looked at the file again. Someone from the Lownes family.

Oh. I thought by the time she came here they'd figured out it wasn't her.

There hadn't been an autopsy, I see, and since from what you said people had identified her in the hospital, even if incorrectly, no one would have been trying to figure out if she was someone else.

So how come the Lownes family moved her to another funeral home?

It's in Bardstown. That's where she's from, it says. Probably had buried other members of the family. It's not uncommon. In times of grief, people like to have something familiar. It can help enormously.

But why would she have come here first?

Perhaps because of the woman's boyfriend. He was local, you said? He probably knew our name, and he'd have called the family, and they'd have made their own arrangements. Fairly standard. Hospitals don't like to keep bodies too long.

I got the feeling he was telling the truth, but I had to push, nonetheless.

I'm sorry to ask, I said. But Hapsburg had some problems before.

We did, he said, his face paling through his tan, exactly as if he were passing away before me. Or perhaps I should say, *they* did, he said. That was before my time. Thankfully. And I can assure you nothing like that is going on here now.

Nothing like what? I said.

No unauthorized trade in body parts. Not a single person who worked here before remains on the staff. I wouldn't allow it, he said, his voice deeper, his back straighter, his demeanor intimidating. *Where had that come from?* I wondered.

As if in answer, he said, My uncle's body disappeared during that whole thing. Every single person who was involved in it should have been locked up. They still should be, he said, and closed the folder and glared at me, so that I wondered if he'd connected my face with the scandal. I hoped not. He seemed a kind man, a good man, not one I'd want to think poorly of me, though even as I had it the wish struck me as absurd.

* * *

Mr. Hapsburg's moral certainty disconcerted me. Outside, the wind had picked up—a stop sign banged on its tilted post—and I leaned into it, digging through my purse for my keys, which was why I didn't see anything at first, even when I was standing right next to the car. But when I did see it, I felt exposed, alone on the prairie with the tornado descending.

My initial response was to drop my keys and glance around for someone watching. They had to be, I thought—they must have wanted to see this time if they'd truly scared me—but no one was lurking, no one standing beside a car to note my reaction before climbing in and taking off. Then I began to tremble, my stomach to heave. A woman's hand, the right one, with long thin fingers and manicured nails, lay centered on my driver's seat.

7

Call the cops, I thought, and then thought better of it; Joan didn't need more reasons to doubt me, and I wondered if that was what my stalker wanted: whatever time I spent tangled up with the legal system was time I couldn't spend chasing Lia. It wasn't Lia's hand—no fleur-de-lis tattoo, the fingers too long—but I couldn't help worrying that she'd been cut up too.

I wasn't going to tell Mr. Hapsburg, either; whatever suspicions he'd harbored about me before, this would only confirm. So I covered the hand with a blue handkerchief and stood with it clasped within my own, its chill telling me it had been refrigerated until recently. What was I to do with it? I couldn't throw it out, and before long, it would begin to smell, so I decided to get a cooler and some ice.

After scrubbing my hands raw in the dirty bathroom sink, I stood by my trunk, ostensibly to fill the car with gas but really to keep an eye on passing traffic. Someone was watching me, I was sure of it, they had to be to know that I'd been eating lunch with Amed, then meeting with Joan and Mr. Hapsburg, but either they were very good at what they did or I was a poor amateur sleuth, because by the time the forty dollars of gas had been pumped, I hadn't picked out my shadow. Or rather, I'd picked out dozens of followers, which meant that I had nothing.

I called the Bardstown funeral parlor as I drove home, tired and afraid, the back of my thighs sticking to the seat, windows open in an unsuccessful effort to clear the remaining skunk smell out of the car, relentlessly checking the mirror to be sure I wasn't being followed, only to get a machine. I asked them to contact me, but the longer it took to trace Lia's journey, the less likely it was that I'd find her, so my mood was both fragile and sour when I reached home and found Amed sitting on the front steps, holding a wilted bunch of lavender-wrapped sunflowers.

I rolled my window down and said, Amed, what are you doing here? A part of me still wondered if he was behind all that had happened, but if he sensed anger in my voice, he skipped past it.

I came to apologize, he said. For how I ended our lunch.

Smooth, I thought, as he'd made it sound as if we'd been on a date rather than accidental companions, and *that* made it seem as if I should give him another chance. But if I was too tired to figure out a correct response, if I was bitter about having to take and pay for the drug tests—especially since Joan had *never* before required a Level Two—and if I felt awful after seeing Mr. Hapsburg and scared about what had happened to my car and by the hand, those weren't because of Amed, those were because of me. Because of *my* past. Still, the whole thing seemed off. It was so hard to get out of the car in the sticky heat, I felt as if I was made of a heavier element than everything around me, something far more susceptible to the pull of gravity. But finally I did.

What the hell happened to your car? he said.

An accident, I said, not wanting to discuss it. How did you know where I lived? I asked, retrieving the squeaking cooler as if it was the most normal thing in the world.

The wonders of the Internet, he said.

You *are* stalking me, I said, my anger unmistakable, and slammed the trunk closed. Or was it fear?

Hardly, he said, holding out the flowers. I had no other way of apologizing to you. I'd have called, but I don't have your number, and if I was stalking you, I wouldn't have sat on your front steps.

That sounded reasonable. After all, I was tired and on edge, and none of it was his fault, so I gave him my best smile and said, Amed, it's nice of you, but I'm really beat, and I think you should probably just go.

You know, he said, I work in a hospital, and your skin is a funny color.

What? I said, baffled by his insult.

Yes, he said, stepping closer. And your eyes. He shook his head. You look like you need a good meal and a night off. If I were you, that's what I'd plan for. Can't take a chance it'll turn into something worse. Lucky for you, I'm a good cook.

I laughed with relief. He was right. The shock of Lia's death, the sleepless night, the worry and fear, it was all catching up, and I wanted to feel safe now, to be in the company of someone who liked me, even as I knew it might be a mistake.

I rested the cooler on the front steps, slid the key in the lock, and said, All right. I'll invite you in, on one condition. You're not a psycho.

Uh, no, he said. I'm not. Though I'd hardly be likely to tell you if I were.

Great, I said. Now that we've got that established, come on in. You look thirsty and your flowers are dead.

He inspected them. They didn't hold up too well in the heat, did they?

God no. No point in even trying to revive them. Inside, I put the cooler on the kitchen counter and said, Here, and took the flowers. Thanks, I said, that was really sweet. But now that we've got that out of the way, I'm going to toss them.

After I did, I said, How about some of that iced tea you were so quick to serve me earlier? Can I return the favor?

Sure he said, glancing at the bare walls of the kitchen and dining room. I like what you've done with the place. Looks as though you're really planning to stay.

I laughed, because the truth was I hadn't done anything. No pictures on the walls, no knick-knacks scattered on shelves, nothing on the counters aside from a blue bowl filled with fragrantly overripe peaches; it might have been a blank slate for a photo shoot. I didn't bother explaining that I'd been making enough money from work to buy the place until the scandal hit, and then, when I lost my job, didn't trust that the thirty thousand dollars I'd saved up for furniture and fixings might need to go to a lawyer. Some of it had, and the rest I was keeping for a rainy day.

Really, he said. If you vanished, I don't think anyone would notice.

Okay, I said. I'll buy some pictures. Which made me think of the Derby pictures in Mrs. Hopper's office, which made me think of Lia and our infield trips.

Listen, Amed said. I don't have your number. He pulled out his phone. You could rectify that right now, he said, and I thought how strange it was to be hit on in the midst of thinking about a missing body, but I gave it to him, and the glass of tea, which he rolled over his forehead. Ah, he said. That's nice.

Outside, the weather had shifted again, the temperature climbing back into the nineties, the air quivering with heat waves and smelling of coming storms. Hold on, I said. I'll be right back, and ran the cooler down to the basement, where I tucked it under some towels in a dark corner by the washing machine.

When I came back up, Amed was still holding the iced tea. He drank it in a single long swallow, and I found myself admiring his throat again and poured him another, partly because he was thirsty and partly because I wanted to see it again. When he was done he said, May I sit? and pulled out one of the kitchen table chairs. *Say nothing about the hand,* I kept thinking. I had a brief, urgent desire to weigh it, but

I knew my mind was warped by grief, by lack of sleep. As I sat across from him, I hoped my face showed none of it.

Amed said, You've got one picture in here. Who's that with you?

It was of Lia and me at the beach, which I'd brought with me to look at while I ate breakfast.

Lia, I said. My best friend.

Lia what?

Lia Stefanini.

I'm guessing she means a lot to you. What's she like?

As sweet as carrots, I said, not wanting to correct his tense, to tell him she was dead. He laughed.

I laughed too, which surprised me. Where should I start? I asked, and then, without waiting for an answer, told him how we'd met.

Eighth grade, I said, both of us new to town, and she had a blue streak in her blonde hair, a few strands, and walked into homeroom late with such confidence that I hoped she'd sit beside me. And her perfume! A Chanel, I later found out. Far more sophisticated than anything any-one I knew wore, even up north.

You're from Indiana? he said.

I laughed. No. *North* north. New York.

Oh, okay. Thought your accent was a bit different. Go on.

So I did, for half an hour. When I stopped, the light had changed—evening now, the sky a marbled marine blue, the clouds so low they seemed to scrape the roof—and so had the room's mood. I'd laughed, I'd cried, I'd mimicked Lia's voice and mannerisms, I'd told Amed about her parents (though not what had happened to her father), and by the end of it I missed her so much it was as if we'd stayed best friends through all the years. I felt a fraud and a failure, I wanted to run, to yell, to sing, and I seemed to have passed through every stage of grief in one short span, grief for her shortened life and for my loss, because grief always has a self-reflexive streak, that vision of what we'll never again behold. And now, I'd finally moved to a new stage of grief, one I hadn't realized existed. Watching a vein pulse in Amed's amazing neck, I'd found the part of grief containing lust.

I wasn't sure how much I trusted him, I was certain it was all too fast, but I didn't want to listen to the warning voice inside my head—to Lia, telling me to slow down—instead, I craved distraction and pleasure, desired to be a body and nerves and nothing more, not thoughts, and certainly not emotions. In the long hours since I'd heard of Lia's death, I'd been nothing *but* emotions, and my heart felt so raw now it might have been sandpapered.

Amed also seemed to understand the lust in grief. I almost bit through his shoulder when we first started kissing: I wanted my mouth everywhere. He wanted it too, so I tasted the skin behind his knees and on his thighs and the mushroomy scent of his cock. His mouth tasted of tea and his lips were soft, his tongue insistent and probing. I pushed him down on the table and straddled his face, gripping him with my thighs and reaching back to stroke him whenever I sensed his attention might flag, and as I started to come, my stomach warming, he rolled me over and stood me up and slid inside me slowly, inch by inch by inch, gripping my hips so tightly that I couldn't get him to move more quickly, even as I tried to buck back against him, wanting to be consumed. And then I was.

After, I dragged him to the bedroom where we made love again, more slowly, attentive to time and tension. At one point only his shoulders and heels were touching the bed, his mouth open in a perfect O, and he growled with pleasure; if I'd been just a touch better, I probably could have made him levitate. He returned the favor, cupping his hands under my buttocks and drinking from me as if I were a bowl, and outside the storms began, huge rolling rounds of thunder that shook the house; I seemed to shake in concert with them, to shudder and arch and moan.

Later, I lay with my head on his furry chest, face turned to the window, where the sky was the richest shade of royal blue, shading into a purple-charcoal as I watched, shifting at last to indigo and black, the black shattered by bolts of lighting, in which the swaying trees stood out in sharp relief. The air smelled of burnt sugar and the rain came, pounding on walls and the tin roof, gusts of thrown gravel.

* * *

We slept, we woke, we fucked again, Amed behind me, urgent and rough, my fingers cupping him, my nails raking him, the lightning showing him in flashes, as if he was moving in some kind of slow-motion movie. It made me dizzy.

Holy fuck, Amed said, lying back when it was over, breathing heavily. You *do* know your anatomy.

My ardor cooled and a psychic distance formed between us, a small deep canyon opening in the bed. I stood and grabbed the nearest bit of clothing—his shirt, it turned out, and, as his pants were next to them, surreptitiously, feeling guilty even as I did it, I checked each of his pockets for a knife—and said that I heard my cat crying and headed through the doorway. Luckily Orlando came as soon as I called him from the blowing darkness, after which I went downstairs again to check on the cooler. The hand was there, resting in the melting ice like a joke hand, which would reach up and grab for mine as soon as I tried to touch it.

The floor creaked above me, so I shut the squeaky lid and recovered the cooler with towels and old nightgowns, then hurried upstairs, where I busied myself in the kitchen, feeding Orlando, hoping that Amed would take a hint and get dressed and come out to join me, at which point I could go back and dress myself completely. I didn't feel as awkward as I would have post–drunk sex, but it was close, as what we'd done so quickly felt both intimate and peculiar, as if I'd asked a stranger to floss my teeth.

Soon Amed appeared in pants and one sock—making me laugh, which helped—and when I chastised him for texting, he blushed and slipped the phone into his pants pocket. It made me like him again, feel more forgiving.

Apologies, he said. I'm all yours. Orlando? A Shakespearean cat?

No, I named him after the city I found him in, I said, and soon we were talking about why. I'd been transporting butts to a medical conference for plastic surgeons, practicing butt reduction and Brazilian lifts. I'll tell you, I said. Watching them? You don't want surgeons practicing on the living. Some of the butts they created were just awful.

I liked Amed's laugh. It made me want to hear it more. Anyway, I said, as I was driving them down there, I was terrified a cop was going to pull me over and then I'd have to try to explain to him what I was doing with all those frozen butts.

Yeah, Amed said. And the conference organizers wouldn't have been happy if you showed up with rotting samples. Probably would have ruined your career.

Well, I said, moody again, maybe that wouldn't have been such a bad thing.

Are you crazy? he said. All that money you must have been making? You wouldn't have wanted to give that up, would you?

Not then, no. I bought this house with what I was earning. But afterward, in retrospect, I wish some cop *had* stopped me.

Really? he said. Why?

Instead of telling him, I offered him something to eat. You like eggs? I said.

Not going to tell me, eh? he said, picking up on my elision.

Smart man. And I'm a decent cook.

All right, he said. I'm better than decent, so let's see what's on the menu. He opened the fridge. Sausage too, it looks like, and spinach. Jeez. You've got a lot of it. Were you entertaining Popeye recently?

I elbowed him in the gut.

Oof, he said. The lady's tough.

I'll poach the eggs, I said, and you handle the sausage.

I'll do a tomato hollandaise sauce, he said, and a sauce like that deserves something better than just sausage. Got any cooked potatoes? He poked around in the fridge. Here we go. Sausage hash, then. He pulled out the potatoes and some carrots, the butter, a green pepper. Gentlemen, he said, start your engines.

I put on some zydeco music. To his raised eyebrow, I said, It sets the mood.

Soon the kitchen smelled of the browning pork and onions, the pepper and carrots. Amed's face shone in the stove light, my arm grew tired as I whipped the egg yolks and water, my stomach growled. Amed laughed and reached over and unbuttoned my shirt down to my navel.

Hey, I said, swatting at him. Hands at home.

They are, he said. That's my shirt. Besides, he said, and scooped up some of the clarified butter with his thumb and anointed one of my nipples, which instantly grew erect. You're one of those people who look good with food on them, New York.

Oh? I said, What should I call you then? Where are you from?

Louisville, he said. Born and raised.

Well, Louisville, I said. Better check your hash. It's starting to smoke.

Fuck! he said, lifting the bottom with the spatula and finding it burnt.

Don't worry, I said. Scrape off the bottom. I'll never tell.

He was sweating, which gladdened me—he wanted to please me—and once he plated the dish and poured the sauce and wiped the edge with a dish towel my stomach was gurgling with desire, but he had me sit at the table and dashed outside.

What are you doing? I said when he came back, but he held up one finger and told me to close my eyes.

I did. He opened drawers and ran water, snipped something with a scissors, told me at last to look. On the plate a sprig of mint was folded around a bright orange nasturtium, and I thought, *No one who would do this could be bad.*

The sauce was as lustrous as ivory, buttery and lemony at once, the diced tomatoes a perfect finish. It was so good I wanted to eat it by itself.

Where did you learn to cook like that? Your mother?

Sullivan University.

The cooking school? How'd you end up in medicine?

I'm good with a knife.

Ha ha, I said.

Debt.

Wait. You went to med school because you wanted to get *out* of debt?

He laughed. That would be pretty dumb, wouldn't it? No, I work in the morgue to make extra money.

Oh, I said. I just thought that, well, the way you were dissecting that foot.

He shrugged. It's not that I'm not interested in med school. It's just that I don't now how to get there. My college grades aren't that good. And an associate's degree in culinary arts doesn't really meet the premed requirements. But it's pretty fascinating, you know? Watching the surgeons come down and get parts to practice on. And I'm better than most of the anatomy students at dissections. They usually pay me to take the brains out, since they're not graded on extraction, and they want to make sure they've got a brain they can work with, and some of the surgeons pay me to help them too, when they need a prosection. I'm taking an A&P class now. It's hard, and it kind of sucks, but it's better than cooking school.

I gathered the plates and put them in the sink. What was the worst thing about cooking school?

The worst? Other than ending up with a bucket-load of debt? Well, that's easy. This one instructor. She'd worked in some really good kitchens, but she was Gordon Ramsey on steroids. Made every single woman in my class cry, and a lot of the men. When we went for drinks, we talked endlessly about what we could do to get back at her. Nasty evaluations didn't work, humor either.

One day she was riding me about how I'd mishandled cheese, just screaming abuse in my ear, and she followed me into the walk-in cooler, and somehow, as I was getting down a bucket of feta, I managed to unseal the lid. I swear it was an accident. All the liquid slopped out over her, soaking her instantly. It smelled awful, and from her perspective, the worst part was her chest.

Big, he said, holding his hands in front. A drenched bra. No matter how many times she changed her chef's whites, the bra soaked through it. She couldn't take it off, she smelled awful, and all day it was like she was in a wet-tee shirt contest. She was convinced I did it on purpose.

I wish. My classmates bought me celebratory drinks, but for the rest of the semester she rode me mercilessly. Almost made me quit. Ended up losing fifteen pounds, and I don't think I learned a thing. By the end of it, my confidence was shot.

Why would they let someone like her continue to teach?

His face changed. Well, she doesn't anymore.

Good, I said. Because of you?

No, he said quickly, not looking at me. Not me.

Well, you got your confidence back. You know your way around a kitchen.

He waved his hand dismissively. For all the good it's done me, he said. How about you, what's your worst story?

Probably Dr. Giorgio, I said, too quickly, wanting it to be true.

The anatomy professor? Was he one of those asshole docs?

Not at all. A nice guy. But he had a thyroid condition and he was bug-eyed. Once he was explaining a prosection and he wasn't watching where he was going. He walked into a doorway and one of his eyes popped out.

Jesus.

Dropped right into his hand, hanging by the optic nerve. Oh, darn, he said. Hate it when that happens.

I lost it. I'd already done hundreds of autopsies by that point, but it was just so weird. For months after, I was afraid he'd have it pop out again.

I can see that, Amed said. It's making my stomach queasy now.

Sorry. But it's not as if you don't see weird things in the morgue.

Tell me about it. Tattoos. On the eyeballs, inside of lips, the roof of the mouth. One guy came in with a tattoo of hair.

It was as if he'd known what button to push. Odd tattoos. McDonald's, Carmine Semple, Lia; I still didn't want to talk about it so I got up and rinsed the plates in the sink.

Let's leave the dishes for later, he said, helping me, piling up the clattering silverware, bending suddenly to pull one breast into his mouth and sucking until the nipple was taut, my thighs growing hot.

Here, I said, scratching his chest. Let's go back into the bedroom.

* * *

Later, in bed, sore, I checked my phone and found no messages, which surprised me, as I'd expected the funeral home in Bardstown to have called. Awake beside me, Amed trailed his fingertips down my smooth inner thigh, then thumbed his phone to life and said, I've got a couple of messages. He sat up to listen.

Shit, he said, standing after one. I have to leave. Work. He grabbed his pants and underwear. The morgue. Something always goes wrong there.

He ran the shower, leaving the door open, and I looked at the picture of Lia and me in front of the tobacco barn, the home screen on my phone. *Something always goes wrong.* Too true. And at times not just something but everything. In my case that had started when I'd stripped Lia's father's body.

I was just an assistant on the job. The leader got the cadaver while I prepped the table, and Julie was funny about recoveries; she never wanted to see the face, so she always covered it with a bag. When she brought it out and I didn't recognize him, we started with the skin, trash-talking as usual about who could do the most the fastest, and when it came time to harvest the back I was really into it.

But once we flipped him I knew it had to be Mr. Stefanini. No one else could ever have had Rush Limbaugh's face tattooed on his ass. I'd never seen the tattoo, of course, yet the family always joked about it, so I stopped, but then I figured, Well, I've already started, and he must have signed the donor papers, so this must have been what he wanted. Skinned his back and his legs, and then we opened him up and took his spine.

Later, back in the office, long after we'd sutured him up and rebagged him and washed everything down, I checked the paperwork. They had the wrong age for him, the wrong name. When I told Julie, she said, Listen, it's just a screwup. Someone further up the food chain mixed up the paperwork. We'll probably be back at the same funeral home tomorrow for a Mr. Stefanini.

But we weren't, then or ever, and if at first I couldn't decide how best to tell the Stefaninis, after the funeral it seemed impossible, and then too much time had passed for me to do it without seeming either cowardly or evil. I was certainly the first, though I hoped not the second, so I tried not to think about it, unsuccessfully, as the mistake haunted most of my days. And after news of what I'd done to Mr. Stefanini came out in the papers, though not its accidental nature, and after I became to readers far and wide a coldhearted corpse skinner, willing to mine even those I loved for money, with or without permission, Lia and Mrs. Stefanini had no desire to hear my explanation. And I couldn't blame them.

Yet now I was looking for his daughter. I owed it to Mrs. Stefanini to find her, no matter what else might happen, so when Amed emerged from the bathroom, toweling off his dark hair, I said, Listen. I might need your help.

Doing what? he said, standing over me, unselfconsciously naked.

When I met you in the morgue? I was there looking for a body. A friend's body, I said, going on quickly. She's gone missing.

Who is it? he asked, slipping on his underwear.

I explained about Lia, about how she'd been operated on and died, all while under the wrong name.

Lia? he said. Your friend? The one you were telling me about? Why didn't you tell me she had died?

Because I didn't want to believe it, I said. Nor did I want to talk about that, so I held up my phone. But I've got a lead on her. Down in Bardstown.

Bardstown? he said, his voice changing. Why down there? He zipped up his pants and I told him what I'd learned, that Lia's boyfriend had arranged for the Hapsburg

Funeral Home to pick her up, and that sometime in the following days she'd been transferred from Hapsburg to a different funeral home, thirty miles away in Bardstown, when
they still thought she was Cindy Lownes.

Wow, Amed said. Good that you traced it that far.
What happened then?

Still waiting to hear.

He was almost dressed. When he finished he put a hand
on my shoulder and said, Elena, if you need help tracking
her down, call me.

Really? I said. You don't think I'm awful, for not having told you?

No, he said, and bent to kiss my forehead. You needed time to trust me. I understand. It's fine. I'm glad you
finally did.

I hugged his trunk so hard I thought he might bruise.

* * *

The air outside was clear and brisk after the passing storms,
the dawn a ragged pink chalk line to the east. Birds sang
and fireflies floated in the still air. I walked him down the
drive to his van, our footsteps crunching over the gravel, my
bare shins rubbing against the long damp grass, everything
smelling of water. The van was a peculiar yellow-green,
the hydrangeas beyond it flattened after the torrential rain,
their heavy powder-blue heads bent deferentially to the
ground. I kissed him, watched as he opened the back door
and pushed aside a familiar-looking plastic gallon bottle of

clear liquid and fished out a different pair of sneakers from a plastic bag.

Work shoes? I said, and he nodded. I knew the drill. You worried that the smell of death clung to you so you kept your work clothes outside, to seal off that part of your life. Not that it succeeded, as you came to feel, given enough time, enough dead to work on, that an essential part of you—some ineradicable kernel—had gone rancid.

After Amed tossed his other shoes in the back, I saw several pairs of woman's riding boots and stepped closer to inspect one. They looked like Zanottis. Scuffed uppers, a worn-down left heel.

I felt chilled, and when he turned to say good-bye, I dropped my chin and let him kiss my offered forehead. His lips seemed to burn, though I knew I was only imagining it.

Now get some sleep, Elena, he said, and squeezed my shoulders with both of his strong hands. You need it. As much as I'd like to, I don't want to have to come back here again to fuck you into unconsciousness.

Clever comebacks sprang to mind, but I said nothing, desperate to have him go.

8

As if they'd been waiting for him to leave, the Bardstown funeral parlor called as soon as Amed's taillights disappeared.
I didn't want to answer, not now, but I had to. A Mrs.
Browning. Please, she said, call me Myrtle, in the subdued
empathetic tone of someone with years experiencing grief.

Troubled by doubts about Amed, I made myself focus and explained the mix-up with the body, that Cindy
Lownes was really Lia Stefanini, and that I was trying to
recover Lia's body on behalf of her family.

Yes, she said. We knew about that. But there must be
some other mistake.

Well, I said, I assume at this point the Lownes family
knows that their daughter *isn't* dead?

They do, Ms. Kelly, Myrtle said, but this was all cleared
up two days ago. That's why I'm surprised. The body was
already recovered by the Stefanini family.

What? I said, shocked. I'm sorry, I said. Could you say that again?

Yes, certainly. Here, hold on, let me look it up.

While she typed, I wondered how such a thing was possible. Mrs. Stefanini was unlikely to have tracked down Lia and not told me, unless she was exacting a sick revenge. Impossible, in the midst of her own grief.

Yes, here it is, Myrtle said. The deceased was here for less than twenty-four hours before the mix-up was straightened out and QPR came for it.

QPR?

QPR Delivery Services, she said. They're from Southern Indiana.

Have you used them before? I asked.

We hadn't. We tend to work with a few contractors, but from time to time another company gets involved. And the call came directly from the family.

From Mrs. Stefanini?

No, I'm sorry, she said. I should have said before, the Lownes family. From a Robert Lownes.

But why was Mr. Lownes calling? It wasn't his daughter.

Mr. Lownes told me he was dealing with it because the Stefaninis were still reeling from the shock. He was a very nice man, I recall. You could just tell from his voice. Mr. Lownes said that, in their great relief, they wanted to help their daughter's friend's family.

They were friends? Lia and Cindy?

According to Mr. Lownes.

I asked, And they transported the body to . . .?

I'm sorry, she said, it says only TBD.

Okay, thanks, I said, and as I was about to hang up, I thought of something.

Myrtle? I said. Have you told the police this?

The police? Why would they be involved? Was there some kind of crime?

No, I said. It's just that Mrs. Stefanini told me that she'd talked to the police, once the body went missing.

It's gone missing? Myrtle said. When?

I don't know, I said. That's why I called you. I'd hoped you still had it.

No, I'm sorry. I wish I did. But here's the contact info for QPR, if you want it.

I wrote down the number and thanked her, and she said, I do hope this gets cleared up soon. I'd hate for there to be a problem.

I said I hoped so too and once I was off the phone I dialed QPR and learned it was not a working number. Nothing on the Internet either, nor in the phone book when I went old school. I spent longer searching than I probably should, as it felt good to have something to do, to distract myself.

Finally I thought of calling Mrs. Stefanini, but decided there was little point in doing so. What would I tell her, after all? That her daughter had been taken from the morgue at University Hospital to the Hapsburg Funeral Home, and from there to another in Bardstown where an unknown company from Southern Indiana had picked it up, knowing now who they had and doing so in Mrs. Stefanini's name? No. I wanted to bring her something tangible, the body or its location, not to increase her grief. So I would wait until I knew more.

Still a coward. But then I told myself, What of it? Was it so terrible not to want to cause her more pain, to hope she could forgive me for what I'd done to her husband if I returned her daughter?

Crying to be let outside, Orlando woke me from my reverie, darting into the warming air as soon as I opened the door. The cicadas faded as the birdsong rose, and like Orlando I wanted to move, to do something, but what? I needed some way to get the chain of events after Bardstown clear.

The police were out—they hadn't done a thing, from what I could tell, and the fear of having violated my probation was too strong to overcome—and unless Myrtle was lying, the only other option was the Lownes family, who weren't likely to be up this early.

The only clean coffee mug left had UPSALE! printed on its side, one of the last gifts Lia had ever given me. From the start it had depressed me, but I'd pretended it was a favorite, and after we stopped talking I kept it as a reminder. Of what I'd lost, of how it had been my fault.

She was working in sales at a wine store, where her boss bored her with hourly motivational talks. *Live in an attitude of gratitude! Turn it on and turn it up! Impossible is nothing!* His favorite term was *Upsale*, which he used whenever he wanted to move certain bottles. *If people ask for your recommendations, it's time to upsale the ones with the biggest markup.*

Lia had laughed about it, suggesting I use it too. BTBs,

she'd said. Bone tendon bone, right? Let's upsale the btbs this week, half a dozen for the price of five!

After that, we jokingly traded weekly sales figures, until one night, back at her apartment following hours at a bar, she'd changed into her pajamas and sat on the couch, spooning in mouthfuls of Graeter's butter rum ice cream while watching the news. The lead story was the follow-up to an accident, a university student drowned when a river barge ran over her crew shell.

Did you get in on that? Lia said.

I had, though I pretended not to have heard Lia, to be absorbed in the reporting, but the truth was that in order to get the body, I'd said I was a relative and altered her paperwork. At the time, I felt justified. Her family had signed off on organ donation, and I told myself they'd simply forgotten about the harvesting of tissues, a small mistake I was only rectifying. And a common one. Of the eight thousand deaths in the city every year, five thousand were suitable donors, but only a couple hundred ever signed off on tissue donation because the world of tissue donation was seamier than that of organs.

I was only balancing things out, I'd told myself then, but I knew I was trying to convince myself. And, after, I knew that the moment I began lying to my friend was the moment I should have stopped.

Upsale that, I thought.

Then I had another thought and called Myrtle Browning back.

Myrtle, I said, can you talk to the tech and ask him about the guy who picked up the body? If the QPR driver gave his name? Also, could you ask if he had an ambulance or a hearse?

I already spoke to him, Myrtle said. After your call I was so upset I just had to figure this out. He couldn't remember much about the driver. Tall, he said, well over six feet, wearing overalls, a stubbled face. I'm sorry I don't have more. No name. She hesitated for a moment and then went on. But it had to be someone who knew about the body and the mix-up, right? I mean, no one would risk this if they didn't know something about what had happened. It would be too easy to get caught.

The driver, I said. You sure the tech didn't notice anything else about him? Tattoos, maybe? Scars? If he was black or white?

White. He was wearing overalls and gloves and a turtleneck, despite the heat.

Thank you, Myrtle, I said, not surprised about the turtleneck. That helps.

And it did, as I was pretty sure it described Belmont Pitken, Lia's last boyfriend.

Please tell me what you find out, Myrtle said. I want to make sure nothing like this ever happens again.

I will, I said. I promise.

I heard her flipping a page of paper. She said, Oh, and the tech told me it wasn't a hearse or an ambulance, it was a van. Sort of an ugly shade of greenish-brown, he said. That's why he remembered it.

He had a van? I said, thinking of Amed. Not quite the same color, but still, an odd enough one for someone to notice. And Amed had those riding boots, the gallon bottle of Optisol. If he was involved, it wouldn't be surprising that he used sex to find out what I knew; I'd used everything to get what I wanted, in my day. Still, I hoped it wasn't true.

I thanked Myrtle and hung up and, before I could stop myself, made another call. Early still, but Buddy never slept much.

When he answered, I said, Buddy, I don't think I'm coming in today.

What? he asked. Why not? He cleared his throat. Is this related to that personal thing you wouldn't tell me about?

It is, I said.

Are you sick? he said. I can say you're sick when the PO calls.

Sure, I said. Say that. Say that I'm sick.

But you're not, are you?

I couldn't lie to him. For the last three years I'd been doing a good job of not lying, until a day and a half ago when Mrs. Stefanini called, and I didn't want to revert to that earlier version of myself. So I told him the truth. No, I said. I'm not sick. But there's something I have to do.

He was silent so long I could hardly bear it. At last I said, Buddy?

I'm glad you told me the truth, he said, his voice sounding very far away, as if during the pause we'd been traveling different directions in space. But I'm going to do the same. When your PO calls, I'll have to tell her. I'm sorry. I can't lie to her.

I know, I said. I don't expect you to.

Which didn't mean that I wasn't hoping you might. But I was running out of time and the Stefaninis deserved an answer, and it had to come before whoever was trying to scare me off succeeded.

Fuck, I said aloud, as I hung up. You just threw away your future.

Everything felt like it was moving too fast, the day's growing heat and light, the ever-louder sound of the birds, the sickening feeling that Amed knew all along, even as he watched me move above him. My blood, which seemed filled now with tiny metal shards, tearing my body apart as it hurtled toward my stomach.

I had so wanted to Amed to be true. A few friends stuck by me for a while after the scandal. But now? I felt utterly alone.

9

Belmont's Facebook page showed that he still worked the airport's UPS night shift, which meant that he'd be getting off shortly. I had to see him. The QPR driver description matched him exactly, and Myrtle was right: whoever did this knew about the mixed-up names; even the most brazen body brokers didn't steal random bodies. As I showered, I thought about Myrtle's other comments, her desire that this not turn into a problem, and I knew that by *problem* she meant *news story*.

I understood. Newspapers and TV clarified and corrupted; everything became bright and simple. Covering my scandal, reporters noted that feet brought body brokers $3,000 a piece, brains $10,000, elbows $2,500, and that a complete torso fetched $10,000 while an eviscerated one still went for $7,500, and that a six-foot section of skin returned $6,000. But none of the stories detailed the costs of harvesting body parts, or of transporting, storing, or processing them: freezers, the filing fees for death certificates and cremation permits and all the other paperwork associated with death, or of the harvesting tools. That my skin-shaving blades ran $600 a set and lasted only a single cadaver. Nor did they mention that while most of the business was shady, some procured material saved lives, or that working so closely with the dead eventually deadened your response to the world. So I knew why Myrtle didn't want it publicized. A good ghoul story was a big seller, and only partially true. But I was more worried about Belmont, who I hadn't told Mrs. Stefanini I'd introduced to Lia. Why give her another reason to hate me?

Lia and I had been at a bar when Belmont walked in. I'd dated him twice, months before. On our first date, we'd driven thirty miles south of the city, through the beginnings of the knobs to Bernheim Arboretum. A former forestry student, as we walked through the holly grove toward the pines, he explained the way lumberers viewed the woods, pointing to a towering specimen. One large tree is worth more than two smaller ones, he said, and you look for the first major defect like a fork to determine board feet or numbers of logs. It's a resource, not a tree.

All through the picnic, which I'd fixed and he loved, he told me about merchantable heights and chatter marks and flitching, and it all felt oddly romantic, though not much happened other than kissing. But the second date was a disaster, Belmont arriving drunk and belligerent, so much so that, when he stood in the bar doorway, I ducked.

Lia said, All right, what's that about?

Worst mistake ever.

How big of a mistake can he be when he looks like a model?

He's got the brains of a mannequin.

It's not like you planned on marrying him, is it?

Not once he took his pants off.

Oh, she said, disappointed. Mr. Peanut?

Worse. He came naked to our second date. And drunk. And he had a tattoo.

Lots of people do, Lia said. Us included. She flashed the golden fleur-de-lis on the underside of her wrist. Since when does that rule someone out?

It's on his dick, and it's a dragon.

The boy with the dragon tattoo! Lia burst out laughing, so loudly that half the bar turned in our direction, including Belmont, who headed straight for us.

Elena, he said. Your friend has a great laugh. Introduce me.

Her standard brush-off was that men didn't interest her, but she surprised me by saying, Lia. And I can speak for myself, Mr. Dragon.

He did look handsome when he smiled. Yes, he said, and sat beside her. I'm a big dragon man. If you're lucky, you'll get to see why.

Seriously? I thought. *That's your line?*

Soon, Lia was laughing, Belmont buying her scotches.

I said nothing, appalled that she found him interesting, but if someone drew a line, Lia always stepped over it. From curiosity, not combativeness, and Belmont was certainly a curiosity. Still, it was like watching a flash flood destroy everything around you, and I listened until he offered to show her his tattooed stomach just as my phone lighted up, when I waved the phone at them and went outside to take it.

It was the last time I saw Lia, I realized now as I backed out of the driveway, slowly because the AC fogged the windows. By the next day she wasn't taking my calls, and by the day after that, she'd unfriended me on Facebook. Her final text message read: *Tattoos and betrayal: FOREVER.*

The caller had been a reporter, asking for a comment.

On what? I'd asked her.

That the paperwork on the corpses you wrangle is altered or missing, or that some of your corpses have disappeared. That's all going in the story.

What story? I asked, staring stupidly at my narrow, elongated reflection in a sidewalk puddle. As if it might alter things, I toe-tapped the puddle to make my fragile reflection disappear.

The lead story on the six o'clock news tomorrow, the reporter said.

* * *

Outside Belmont's house, I waited in my car, running the air-conditioning. The mostly sleepless nights, Lia's disappearance, what I now suspected about Amed, I felt on the verge of desolation until I heard Belmont's car, its unmuffled engine growing louder and softer as he shifted gears, when I told myself to buck up, that he might lead me to Lia's body. Eventually he pulled to a stop across from me, parking in the long early-morning shadows.

In my corpse-wrangling days, I usually said I was a recruiter, and, if pushed, that I was in the medical field—vague enough for most people. But sometimes, late, at a bar, someone kept pushing, and then I'd admit to everything. Corpse recruiter, I'd say, leaning in, and then, leaning closer, Want to sign up? Belmont hadn't flinched, a type I learned to avoid, but that night I'd agreed to date him. Now I wondered if everything would be different—if Lia would still be alive—had I been wiser, earlier. But I stopped. I'd ruined many things, yet I hadn't ended her life.

When he shut off the engine the sudden quiet in the neighborhood was startling, and he sat a few moments staring out the windshield at the row of parked cars, flaring sunlight lending polish to their dull paint, and the line of camelback houses as alike as Monopoly pieces stretching away into the distance, their U of L and American flags hanging limply in the already oppressive air. At this time of day, this close to the university, almost no one was up and about, students still hungover, children still sleeping, shift workers already laboring at Ford, Toyota, and UPS. A neighborhood I never made much money in, back in my working days.

Then the door creaked open and he climbed out and slammed it shut. I got out of my car, stunned by the sudden heat—in only an hour the temperature must have risen fifteen degrees—and called his name.

He squinted. I'd forgotten his vain refusal to wear glasses. One hand over his eyes like a visor, he couldn't seem to make out who I was.

I know you? he said.

Yeah, I said, walking toward him. Elena Kelly. Lia's old friend?

His body turned rigid. Not my fault, he said. The car and everything. He waggled both hands in front of his stubbled face. I had no idea it was her.

Walk me through it, I said.

I don't owe you an explanation, he said. You're not Lia's friend, you're her *ex*-friend. I heard all about what you did. Why the fuck should I tell you anything?

We both know why, I said, deciding that the best way forward was to make him feel vulnerable.

He rocked on his heels, studying me, then burped. I smelled beer, which I didn't mind. Drunk, he might not pick up that I was bluffing.

He cleared his throat and said, Fine. It's not like you think. I came home from work early and caught her cheating on me. In *our* bed. Some guy she'd met at a bar. A skinny screamer, once I broke his nose. Good thing I didn't have a gun.

Lia, bringing a pickup back to her boyfriend's house? That seemed far-fetched. But it had been three years; she might have changed completely. And she must have changed a lot, to live with Belmont.

I could've handled it if it was some old flame or something. Wasn't. So I tossed her. I think she came back for her stuff and decided to take the car.

What makes you say that?

Because some of her things were *in* the car. Bobblehead dolls from that show she likes. Liked. *The Office*?

If you saw those, why didn't you know it was her?

Because I didn't see them until long after she'd died. The cops impounded the wreck, since it was stolen. But even if I saw it the first day, I wouldn't have guessed Lia was driving. Cindy hated the dolls. She was always after me to get rid of them.

The day before the accident, Cindy tore off their heads, one by one. I lit into her and she told me to go fuck myself, threw the box at me and took off herself. So when the car was gone the next day, it was pretty natural to think it was her.

He produced an open beer from his jacket pocket as a giant UPS cargo plane flew low overhead, heading for the airport, its engine noise deafening, drank, offered me some—which I refused—drained the rest, and tossed the brown bottle on his neighbor's yard. So, after the accident, he said, as the engine rumble subsided. When the hospital called with the description? It made sense. Same height, same hair color, same haircut. Cindy had stolen the car to get back at me.

Now I think that Lia came back, like maybe she wanted to talk again, to apologize, saw the box and figured I'd torn their heads off and that there was no chance for us. Otherwise, why take the car and not put on her seatbelt?

She always wore one, I said.

Not this time. Might be alive if she had. Though maybe

not. He pulled out his phone, thumbed through a couple of screens, held it out to me.

Jesus, I said. The car was a wreck, the driver's door caved in, its roof crushed. A giant seemed to have stomped on it.

This picture doesn't do it justice. That thing was *destroyed*. It's a miracle she even made it to the hospital.

What about her purse? Wasn't it in the wreck?

Someone stole it, he said. The cops' theory is that whoever got there first thought Lia was already dead. Bunch of charges showed up a day or two later. McDonald's, Burger King, two iPods, and four hundred dollars worth of shampoos and perfumes. Must have cleaned out an entire aisle of some Target in Alabama. Someone else on the highway.

Poor Mrs. Stefanini, I thought, fretting at the world's cruelty, that someone would stop only long enough to steal from her dying daughter.

And when did you figure out it was Lia?

After Cindy showed up here again. Scared the shit out of me, I can tell you that. Thought she'd come back to haunt me.

What about Lia's tattoo? Why didn't you see that in the hospital?

Never looked at her wrist. Only uncovered her head when they called me in. She was blonde, you know? The thing is, he said, everything that happened after? Not my fault either.

Bullshit, I thought, but kept my mouth shut; this was what I'd come for.

It's because I thought it was Cindy, and because of my

fucking boss. Cindy was from Bardstown. Her mother said that's where she was going to bury her. I wanted to go to the funeral and her mother wouldn't tell me where it was. Didn't want me there, she said. Blamed me for her daughter's death.

But you were going to go to her funeral anyway, I said, my implication clear: *You're an even bigger ass than I thought.* He didn't pick up on it.

Just because she didn't like me doesn't mean she's right. Lots of people don't. Anyway, he said. People don't think straight when they're grieving, you know? And I lost my job. Missed a couple of days because of the stuff with Cindy, and when I tried to explain, my boss wouldn't listen. I was trying to help Cindy's family and that bitch went and fired me. If she hadn't, none of this would have happened.

So, then Cindy walks back into the house and at first I almost pissed my pants, thinking she was a ghost. Then I smelled her perfume, and I thought, No, ghosts don't wear perfume. And even though we never had a great thing going I mean, it was never like me and Lia—I was happy. She was alive. Alive! I knew how happy her mom was going to be. I made Cindy let me be the one to tell her. That woman used to come over here all the time and say I was no good for Cindy. Stand right here on my porch and insult me. And now I was going to be the one to restore her to life. She'd never be able to say another shitty thing to me again.

Did it not go well?

He laughed. She didn't even thank me. Thought I was

being cruel. I had to put Cindy on the phone, and even so she didn't believe it until she got over here. The two of them went off together, and I haven't heard a thing from them since, except when they called about a day later and asked me who was in the car.

And you knew it was Lia.

No. I called the hospital to let them know it hadn't been Cindy, and they connected me to the morgue. I explained what had happened, figuring they'd want to know for their records. The guy I talked to wanted the body back and I saw an opportunity.

An opportunity? I said.

Belmont must have heard my tone, because he grew defensive again. Hey, he said, I'd just lost my job. So yeah, if I could make a couple of hundred bucks, sure, why not? It wasn't illegal or anything. And I knew from everything Lia had told me that you used to make good money doing this.

So you told the guy at the hospital what had happened? How come there's no record of it?

He breathed deeply, hiccupped. The guy at the hospital said it was a Jane Doe. Said he was going to take care of it.

And did you know what that meant?

He shrugged. At that point, I didn't know who it was, so I didn't care. Doesn't matter if you don't believe me, but I didn't. Thought it was just someone who'd stolen the car, someone unlucky, someone no one knew. Figured the police could sort it out. I could probably have guessed, but I didn't want to. I was going to get my money and that would be that, or so I thought. Picked her up in Bardstown and dropped her off back at University Hospital. Three hours later Lia's mom called, asking if I'd seen Lia, and I put two and two together.

He looked at me again. For the record, he said, I told the guy at the morgue right away. Amed. Asked about the body. He'd already sold her.

Christ, I said, feeling gutted. I hadn't wanted to believe Amed was really involved. Sweat burst out under my arms. Why didn't he tell me? I asked.

He knew, Belmont said. He knew from the first moment he saw you.

Wait, I said, as he was heading to his door.

He held it open with one foot. What? he said.

I was thinking of Amed showing up at my table at The Garage, hours after I'd first talked to him. He knew from the moment he met me?

He called me as soon as you left the morgue. Said he was going to keep an eye on you.

Why?

That body is worth a lot of money.

That *body*, I said, was your girlfriend.

Not anymore, he said. Not like that. And when I found out what it was worth, I should have asked for more.

I wanted to be appalled. At me, though, not him, because I knew exactly what he meant. Toward the end of my time as a corpse recruiter, I'd come to see nearly every body as a source of funds. Everybody. Whatever lives and loves those bodies had housed were unimportant in death; the living had urgent need of them. *I* had urgent need of them.

Elena, he said. Just let it drop. Amed's boss is rough.
Don't fuck with him.

I was confused. Dr. Handler? I asked.

This guy didn't sound like a doctor. Called me yester-
day. He's got a voice like ground glass. Told me not to say
a thing to anyone or I'd regret it. And then he offered me
$500 to slash your tires if you came around. So forget it,
okay? It's not worth it.

Now you're protecting me? I said. Right. My mirrors,
my tires, the rear seat, the skunk. And the hand?

Wait, he said. What hand?

Don't even try, I said. A minute ago you were wishing
you'd made more money off your dead girlfriend. And in
order to make whatever you did, you called the Bardstown
funeral home, pretending to be Cindy's father, then drove
down in Amed's van to pick up Lia's body. You knew then
who she was. You didn't find out after.

That surprised him, I could tell. He thought he'd covered
his tracks. I wanted to hurt him, to make him feel some of
the pain Lia's mother was suffering, that I was. To be afraid.

Belmont Pitkin, I said, my voice acid now. Protector of
the downtrodden.

He looked stricken, which felt good. But he rallied.
That tattoo? he said. That fleur-de-lis on your wrist? The
one you two got on your birthday?

This one? I said, showing mine, which he refused to
look at.

Yeah, well, Belmont said. Lia removed hers. It wouldn't
have shown up.

But it would have left a scar, I said, my throat clogging, wanting what he'd said to not be true. I hadn't realized how much hope I'd clung to, that she might still have maintained some affection for me, might have wanted to forgive me even if the time for forgiveness hadn't yet arrived. I wasn't going to let him see me falter.

You wouldn't have noticed the scar, I said, my voice not shaking. It would have looked like a burn, a scar like that.

You're right. She was banged up something awful. Bruises, scratches, cuts. Her face swollen. Dried blood crusted in her ear, twigs in her hair. They'd started to clean her up, but she was still a mess. I doubt the scar would have showed.

I said, And it probably would have faded by then anyway. Three years on, most scars get a lot smaller.

He shook his head again, triumph spreading across his face like an unfurling banner. She only had it taken off a month or two ago, he said.

After the screen door slammed shut, I turned back to my car, feeling like I'd been struck with a crowbar. However awful it was that she'd finally cut me from her life forever, just before she died, what had happened to her after was far worse. That she'd been shifted from morgue to funeral parlor to funeral parlor; that her body had been brokered, sold off into the world of the unprotected dead; that she'd become one of the legion of *the less*, by means of someone who was supposed to care for her, to watch over her. To protect her.

I wanted to despise Belmont, but I couldn't. Not really. I'd done exactly the same thing a thousand times. It didn't matter that I hadn't known the people whose bodies I bought and sold and carved, had never loved or cared for them; someone had. And that had never stopped me, even once.

10

I wanted to hurt Amed, but mostly I was baffled by my naïveté. He'd charmed me into lowering my defenses, yet what was the difference, really, between that and using my own gifts to wrangle the dead? For fifteen years I'd worked this world, and I knew its seamy margins. Whatever had made me think the search for Lia wouldn't flow there?

I imagined all the things Lia had revealed about me to Belmont, confidences and quirks we'd shared that he'd been able to use, to pass on to Amed. That I liked cats, men who could cook, the feeling of a man's hands gripping my shoulders from behind. I entered the hospital through the front door, looking as if I belonged, telling the pudgy security guard I had a relative in the ICU.

Know which floor it's on? he said, smoothing his blue tie, and I nodded without breaking stride. Sixth, I said, and he nodded back and passed his glance to the middle-aged couple behind me, who looked scared and confused. Thankfully, I thought, even as I felt bad for doing so, because it meant he wouldn't turn to watch me slip by the elevators and down to the various basements.

My shoes clanked on the metal stairs, the air warming as I descended. Already I smelled bleach. Two floors down I opened a fire door and stepped into the humming, whirring basement tunnels, following the black line to the morgue again, though I knew my way just fine without it. The scent of formaldehyde, the old constant. This time it made my stomach queasy.

Odds were Amed wasn't here, but what else could I do? I didn't even know his last name. I could find it out with a little investigating, but I didn't want anyone to let him know I was coming. I wanted the truth, and the truth was more likely to spring from surprise, something I knew from experience.

After the reporter had contacted me about the unauthorized sale of body parts, my instinct had been to cover things up, to destroy or alter papers, to sell off the last bits of stored tissue. Mistakes, as they made me look guiltier. And then, once the truth started coming out, everything unraveled. I hoped it would for Amed too. I had only the slightest chance of finding Lia now, as she was no doubt at some surgical conference or had already been stripped for parts, but it was still a chance. Hours mattered, minutes.

I took a deep breath and pushed through the morgue doors. The five doctors huddled around the body froze, as if they'd been caught doing something inappropriate. One of the doctors, holding a needle, worked it through a large open wound on the cadaver's chest. Suturing practice, which I'd seen plenty of times.

After a moment, the doors still swinging behind me, the senior doctor recovered enough to ask, May we help you?

My stomach clenched when he pulled down his face-mask. Dr. Weaver. Years before, he'd asked me out in this very room. The other doctors must have been residents.

Yes, I said, taking a half second to decide whether or not to say hello, unsure which would bring me luck, then going for it. Dr. Weaver, I said. Sorry to interrupt.

It was obvious he didn't recognize me. I'm sorry, he said. If this is a relative, I can assure you we meant no disrespect.

No, I said, not a relative. I'm actually looking for Amed.

Oh, well, there are more bodies in the cooler, he said, perhaps recalling a connection between me and the morgue. But nothing from our dinners, or our trip to Chicago, or our conversations about his father and reincarnation. Were my crimes so awful that people had wiped me from their memories?

No, I said. Amed isn't dead. He works here.

Amed? he said. I don't know him. What's his last name?

I don't know, I just slept with him. One of the residents saved me.

Amed Smith, she said.

She couldn't hold my glance, and I suspected they'd been, or were, lovers.

Is he here? I said.

No, she said, and stared down at the pale, obese body stretched out on the table before her, its head, feet, and hands covered by gray towels.

Dr. Weaver said, The only one down here when we arrived was Dr. Handler. He looked up at the oversized wall clock. Shift change in half an hour. Maybe he'll be back then. And with that he returned to his lesson. See this? he said, pointing out the lower part of the incision with a scalpel. Remember, he said, as I walked past them, you have to handle the tissue gently, to get a result that's both functional and aesthetically pleasing.

* * *

I told myself there was no reason he'd remember me, though I didn't believe it. Who wants to be anonymous? We'd shared something in this very room, and I couldn't keep from feeling snarky. *Do I believe in reincarnation? That had been his opening line. You bet I do. And I hope you come back a roofing nail, as a cow patty, plagued by flies and burned for fuel, as a hemorrhoid. As a corpse no-body wants, laid to rest in a pauper's grave with no stone to mark your passing, as a corpse everybody wants, split and sold off to the corners of the earth, never to be reunited.*

Then Lia's voice calmed me. *Nothing to it but to do it,* she said, so I checked the cooler and glanced at the duty roster for Amed's name. I didn't worry that anyone would ask what I was up to, as I'd learned long ago that the best way to avoid such questions was to look as if I belonged.

Handy, when you're harvesting bodies and permissions aren't always in order.

But Amed wasn't on the schedule, wasn't listed under the dieners or med-techs, nor under the anatomists and coroners. He wasn't listed on the whiteboard either, where a few people's numbers were posted; he seemed not to exist in this world and I'd have wondered if I'd imagined his presence if not for the look on that resident's face. I hadn't been the only one he'd charmed.

Perhaps she could tell me more about him, but when I went back through the autopsy room they were still working, and she studiously avoided my gaze. Too studiously, I thought, when her hand slipped and Dr. Weaver gently chastised her.

Outside there were benches, and I determined to wait for them to troop out; perhaps I could cut her from the herd as she passed. An address, I'd say, that's all I want, nothing crazy. It's just that I left my purse at his apartment and don't have his number. It was possible that she'd believe me, more likely she'd tell me simply to have me gone.

So I sat and waited, trying not to bounce my foot or tap my hand on the bench, to show my nerves. My phone buzzed with a message from Buddy.

She called. For a few moments I stared at it, knowing what it meant.

And? I wanted to write back, but didn't, though it didn't matter. His next one came through right after.

Sorry.

So he'd told her. And Joan would be, what? Happy?

No; she was meticulous, not mean. Some petitioners, certain I'd return to my evil ways, had been unhappy about my job in Danville, but the judge told them his hands were tied: the agreement stipulated that I get a job, not what kind. Yet he did recommend closer supervision than for most on probation, which had been the case, so it was only a matter of time before Joan tried to contact me, another short time before she'd report me for not responding. Which meant that soon the police would be involved, and I didn't see how that would be good for anybody.

Feeling as if I was going to be sick, I stood, wanting to move, wanting air, and there was Amed, walking toward me down the hall. Earphones in, he didn't see me at first, but when he did, he smiled, popped out his earphones, said my name, and spread his arms, as if expecting me to jump into them.

Then the doctors emerged from the morgue and his face changed, whether because of my expression or because he saw the resident who'd been doing the suturing, I couldn't tell. But as Dr. Weaver and the others passed, loudly discussing what they'd just practiced, he turned and began walking. Though I called his name over their bobbing heads, he didn't stop; instead, he walked faster.

I was trapped behind the gaggle of doctors in the narrow, echoing hallway; they only reluctantly parted to let me through. Sorry, I said to Dr. Weaver, after treading on his foot, but I didn't slow, because at every second Amed was moving farther ahead. At the next corner he turned left toward the boiler rooms and by the time I turned the corner he'd already pushed through the swinging doors; I thought

I heard him running. I began to run too, not caring what the doctors thought of me.

I couldn't catch him and I wasn't sure which way he'd gone—beyond the swinging doors the hallway split in two directions—and on impulse I turned left again, then left once more, only to find myself at a dead end, an old short hallway used for storing empty fifty-gallon trash cans. After backtracking, after taking two more rights and passing a startled security guard who was pouring coffee from a battered thermos, I came to a door leading outside and burst through so fast that it banged against the wall before slamming shut behind me.

He was a block ahead, moving quickly, bent forward in the rising wind. I was confident I'd catch him. I had him in my sights and nothing was going to alter that until an old woman in an oversized green raincoat stepped out into the street ten yards away. A truck was coming, which she hadn't seen or heard, and I thought, *Oh no, it can't be*, but I knew it would even as Amed turned the corner up ahead. It wasn't even a choice.

Ma'am! I said, loudly enough to startle her, but my voice froze her rather than freed her, so I grabbed her arm and pulled her back toward the curb, losing a shoe in the process. The truck flipped it down a sewer grate, which seemed impossibly bad luck, and the woman said, Bless you, dear, and wouldn't let go of my hand until I'd agreed to walk her across the street, where I took off the other shoe.

You'll cut your feet, dear, she said, but I told her I'd be all right and headed to the corner, looking for Amed. I didn't see him. Fluorescent-vested workmen in yellow hard hats, staring down into an open sewer grate, bicyclists, deliverymen, a food truck with steam venting from its roof chimney, but no Amed. All down Jackson the plane trees bent east in the wind.

Take it easy, Elena, I thought, and made myself stop and breathe. Where would he have gone? To a car, probably, but then I remembered he'd said at The Garage that he lived nearby, in Butchertown.

Ignoring my bare feet, I passed several medical office buildings, and though I didn't see him I kept walking. Now and then a bit of gravel or a chunk of broken pavement made me flinch, but I pressed on, at every traffic light darting across whichever way was clear, heading north and east, toward Butchertown and the river. Its muddy musk grew stronger, my feet sorer, my back sweatier the farther I went in the sticky air. The charcoal gray sky was low and ominous, a bucket about to open.

On Market Street the restaurants were half-full, the furniture shops and galleries empty, the pavement baking. I could never live here, Lia had always said. No trees. The thought of her spurred me on, past the shuttered glassworks, past the Scratch and Dent store, past new wooden fences smelling of pine enclosing empty lots, past the old stockyards, converted now to an orphanage. Another difference Lia and I had always noticed: up north they were called children's homes, and we could never decide whether the honesty of calling them orphanages was a good thing or merely brutal. I crossed an abandoned, weedy playground, its swings moving in the wind in different rhythms, as if ghostly inhabitants still played there, made my way behind an empty warehouse, and passed down the alley next to an abandoned church with a FOR SALE sign out front. Who would buy a church? Amed had said he lived near a church, but this one had no steeple, no bells.

The city was growing older the closer I got to the river, the buildings turning from stone to brick and from brick to wood, getting lower too, crouching above the water as if trying not to be seen, knowing it might rise and smite them. Floods were rare and irregular but always disastrous and always twinned, first from the deluging rain—twenty-three inches in twenty-four hours once—and then days later as the rain that had pushed on up the Ohio River came back down in the form of flood tides. Weather that had made for good corpse wrangling; that's how I'd once viewed it, which was hard to believe now.

Soon the humid air began to stink; the slaughterhouse, which meant I was getting close. I tried not to breathe in the clinging smell. I kept on past an empty gas station, past glassed and bricked-over coal chutes on the sidewalks outside buildings, past curving railroad tracks half-buried under pavement, and then past a double set of tracks, still in use, ending at the meatpacking plant. A dozen men stood talking on one loading dock in their bloody white overalls. The scent here was overwhelming, so powerful I nearly gagged, but they seemed not to notice. Several of them whistled.

I gave them the finger, which inspired one to shout, Smile, it's not so bad!

No, I yelled, I'm not your monkey, but I was feeling worse and worse: What was the difference between their view of women and mine of the dead? True, I'd never *said* the things men did to demean or demoralize—baby, sugar tits, cockholster—but I'd treated the bodies as if they were mine to exploit, at least at the end, by which time how I'd started didn't matter. It was hard to push on then, but I did, unable to stop myself from checking out my reflection in the dusty plate-glass window of a storefront law office. *I look like this and it draws a whistle,* the inescapable force of that unendingly self-critical gaze.

The first drops of rain spotted the street and cars, the pavement gave off a hot dusty smell. A block later the streets themselves began to change, from pavement to brick and from brick to cobble, as if I was walking back into the city's past—with names like Maple and Elm, trees long-since harvested, giving way to Washington and Adams—and, now, nearly within sight of the river, the presidents in turn giving way to the rural past, Blue Horse Ave. and Nanny Goat Alley. Which led me to the floodwalls, the city's last defense against the rising river.

I passed through an open gate down to where everything would be sacrificed in the event of a flood, to Dream's End Lane, an area of older, smaller, shabbier camelback houses in Upper Butchertown, a place my ear had been attuned to for years. When I worked as a corpse wrangler at CGI, on the wall of my boss's office was a giant, multicolored map of Louisville and its surroundings, and on my first day, Kevin had me stand before it.

Think of the city as a grid, he'd said, his hand sweeping across the map as he explained it. Its northern boundary is the Ohio River. To the east are horse farms, to the south tobacco, to the west corn. The three great Kentucky vices: racing, cigarettes, and bourbon. Farm accidents can be profitable, but you can't count on those. If we get them, they're usually from the corn. The city is where we make real money, and for our purposes, the city goes like this. East is white, south is immigrant, west is black. It's the most segregated city in the country, which makes our lives easier, because we get some of the immigrants, especially the Africans, more of the blacks, and few of the whites. But don't waste any time on the suburbials. Almost never happens.

And north? I asked.

By the river? he said, and rested his hand just below its sinuous blue ribbon, arcing across the map. That's our sweet spot. Butchertown, Smoketown, Rubbertown. Mixed and poor and forgotten. Anytime an ambulance picks up the body in those places, odds are, it's going to be ours. He tapped the orange-colored section encompassing them on the map. Yeah. Listen for those on the radio. You hear those and you think: *money*.

And he'd been right. Whenever police called in a body pickup there, I knew it would most likely become mine. Like the buildings, the area's expiring residents were often abandoned to the fates.

I slowed beneath a mulberry tree to catch my breath, leaned against its rough bark; if I was going to see Amed, I was going to see him soon. I needed to; I didn't have much more left in me. *Please*, I thought, *let me*. Otherwise I'd never find him, or I'd find him too late to have any last chance at finding Lia.

My phone rang—my PO—and I switched it off, feeling as if I'd been kicked in the stomach. I was supposed to answer her call at any hour of the day or night, but at this point it no longer mattered. Still, I felt like crying from frustration, that I'd never be able to outrun my past. I'd set this moment in motion years ago, without even knowing it. The forms I'd altered, the protocols I'd skipped; each of them had helped to bring me here.

It was beginning to pour and just as I was about to give in to despair, the bells in the church in front of me began ringing, its steeple white against the black sky, and I knew—absolutely knew—that I was going to see Amed hurrying around a corner to his apartment. I settled in behind the mulberry tree to wait.

* * *

Half an hour later—the bells sounding once to mark it—thoroughly soaked and having ignored two more phone calls from Joan, I knew I'd been wrong. Wherever Amed was, I'd missed him. I'd been planning to recover Lia's body, wanting to help assuage Mrs. Stefanini's unutterable grief, and believing too that it might be the thing that kept me from going to prison, but that wasn't going to happen. I had no idea where she was and the one person who could tell me had slipped away.

What could I do? Without thinking I shouted out his name. Amed Smith!

Then again, louder, and a third time when nothing happened. I know you're here! I yelled, though of course I didn't. Then I yelled Lia's name, and Cindy Lownes's, and Amed's once more, and added that if he didn't come out right away I was going to call the cops.

A shade twitched on the front window of one of the camelbacks, revealing an old white face, which made me feel foolish, and I ducked again behind the tree.

Cindy Lownes, I thought. That would have been the name written on the file, the one with all the intake info, the stuff the EMT guys had phoned in, the surgeon's notes, the nurse's. The final notes would have consisted of the brain death checklist. *No spontaneous respirations, pupils nonreactive to bright light, corneal reflex absent.* If the box next to *oculocephalic reflex absent* had been checked, that would have meant that the cervical spine was still intact, and *that* would have meant that, had she lived, Lia wouldn't have been paralyzed.

I had no way of knowing, but the possibility made me cry, and for several minutes I sobbed, thinking of my friend dead on the operating table and no one there to mourn her. It was awful, awful too that for days she'd been misidentified and trundled about as someone else, that as her spirit fled this world no one on this side of the divide even knew. And worse that now, even as she'd finally been recognized as Lia, her whereabouts were still unknown, her body likely carved up and parceled out.

I decided to call the police no matter what it would mean for me. Mrs. Stefanini had given me the investigating officer's phone number. I dialed it through blurry eyes, and as soon as someone answered, still sobbing, I repeated the only thing I could, over and over: Amed did it, Amed, he's an asshole.

The cop tried to calm me down and began asking me questions, but the moment my breathing started to come under control, Amed reached from behind me and grabbed my shoulder. I was so scared I felt as if I'd slipped out of my skin and was hovering above the street, watching this lone woman with her stilled vermillion heart, the strange man standing over her.

His grip was so strong it hurt. Hang up, he said. Now.

11

I'll tell you where she is, he said, but you're not going to like it. He ducked under the mulberry branches for shelter, though it really didn't matter, as the wind blew the rain sideways.

Do you know Ricky Mads? Amed said. He used to be a nurse. Southern Indiana. Now he wrangles.

Who's he tied in with? I asked.

Indiana med schools and major medical groups. Glaxo-SmithKline, GE, others. He sends them parts.

That made sense. Parts were easier to work with and to store, and certain specialties were eternally changing; if you could find torsos, knees, shoulders, or elbows, you'd always have a steady stream of income, which meant that Lia's fate hinged on whether some new surgical advance was being touted at a conference. If so, she might already have been cut up in preparation.

Asshole, I said, wanting to slap him. You should have told me from the start.

Sorry, he said. But you know the business. You sign a contract and you have to deliver so many bodies a month. Miss one target and you're out. I needed the money, you know? All that debt? And it's not like my skill set transfers easily. Besides, Mads isn't somebody you want to disappoint.

Where in southern Indiana?

Near Corydon. But listen, I mean it about this guy. He's psycho.

Convenient. If he's crazy, you've got an excuse for not telling me.

I'm not making it up. You can't fuck with him.

Why's that? Does he lie? Manipulate people? Get them to tell him things he wants while pretending to comfort them? While fucking them?

He lowered his eyes. Elena, look.

No, *you* look. He's had my best friend for days, and during all that time her mother has been desperate to find her, afraid of exactly this. You could have put an end to her pain, but you didn't. So do it now. Call him and find out. Tell him we want her back.

Don't you think I wanted to? Christ, Elena, I'm not evil. But the guy's been threatening me from the start.

Threats? Like he'll go to the police? Bullshit. No one like that wants the police involved. He'd get arrested too.

No, like, I'll kill you and burn you in my brother's crematorium.

And you believe him?

Remember that teacher of mine, the one I dumped the feta water on? How she doesn't work at Sullivan anymore? I think I'm the reason. I was working at his brother's crematorium, trying to make some extra money. I worked there for one day. One. He held a dark finger in front of my face.

The place is creepy. Multiple bodies in the same burn, corpses stuffed into old furnaces, dripping body fat running down the concrete floor. And after, sifting out the ashes? That's part of working there too. Looking for gold fillings. I took three showers and, even so, in the morning there was an outline of my body on the sheets. The stuff gets into your pores. No ventilation, no oversight, and no records. I hated it, but the money was good, and I'd probably have kept working there except that during a break I mentioned that story to his brother—it had just happened—and that night I got a phone call from Mads.

This teacher of yours, he said. You want me to mess her up? I could put her in the hospital. I thought he was kidding. But the next day she was mugged and beaten. Her arm was broken in three places, and you know how hard it is to break human bone. So yeah, I believe him. I never went back to the crematorium, and I've never crossed him.

Cross him now. Believe me, if he sent Lia there and her ashes are gone, you're going to have a lot more problems than dirty sheets.

Your funeral, he said and dialed. Not picking up. Maybe he's on another run.

Or maybe you're lying, I said.

He held his phone up so I could read the contact info.

Great, I said. You told the truth. For once. Shut up and let me think.

I could call the cop back, tell him everything and they'd get a warrant, but it would take days—interviews with me, with Amed, another state, another DA; Lia would have vanished. Buddy, my PO, Mrs. Stefanini, Dr. Handler, none of them could help. Really, there was only one way to do this with any speed.

You're going up there to get her back, I said.

He laughed. Right.

You'll go, or I'll call the cops. I've been through what follows. You think Mads is scary? Wait until the press gets ahold of you. And the legal system. By the time they're done with you, you'll wish Mads *had* killed and burned you.

Fine, he said. But I'm not going alone.

Indiana? I said, hesitating because of probation. Leaving the state without permission was the third-worst thing I could do, after alcohol and drugs or associating with felons. In the past three years I'd crossed the bridge to Indiana four times. Once for a concert, twice for dinners, and the last time by mistake, when construction on Second Avenue steered me onto the bridge and across the river. Paranoid, since it was the only time I hadn't asked permission ahead of time, I'd called Joan from the car and explained what had happened. She'd required me to come in for a drug test that time too.

The dinners had been unremarkable, the concert a Nico Stai affair, which I'd gone to since both Lia and I loved him and I thought that Lia might be there, that I might bump into her on neutral ground, that we might finally begin to talk again. I'd prowled every aisle of the concert hall without finding her, another failure—like the trips to Louisville's various farmers' markets, the River Bats games, the walk-arounds outside of raves at abandoned cigarette and leather factories near Churchill Downs after I'd heard she'd started attending them.

If those were pushing it, this was worse; Joan would have me clapped in prison for this alone. But odds were I was already going to prison. So if I was afraid and tired and had no idea anymore what the right thing was, the one thing I *had* to hold on to was the desire to find Lia, to return her to her mother to be properly buried. Everything else just fell away.

All right, I said to Amed, raising my voice to be heard over the rising wind. Fine. We'll go. I looked up at the dark, fast-moving clouds. We'll have to hurry. And I've got a condition. That I leave my phone in your apartment. I'll tell you why later. Just put it there. And don't try running out the back.

I won't. You can come with me if you don't trust me.

Trust you? Funny. And I'm not stupid enough to walk into your apartment without any witnesses.

He looked offended. What kind of person do you think I am?

Oh, I think we both know that.

* * *

Five minutes later, we were in his van, headed west, my chest tightening as we neared the bridge. Amed seemed to notice. I'm sorry, Elena. I really am. But mostly, it wasn't my doing. It was Belmont's.

Right, I said, and snorted. At this point, I think I'd rather listen to Belmont's lies than yours.

He called in your probation violation. I didn't even know about that. He volunteered to make things harder for you.

Well, unlike you, he's pretty capable. Now just shut up and drive.

Neither of us said a word all the way to the Sherman Minton Bridge, which had both levels of its double decks packed, all the cars coming from Indiana with their lights on; we crossed it slowly, a dark wall of rain speeding toward us and blinding me as it hit the windshield, blotting out the river. The river. I could go weeks, months, without smelling it or seeing it or even knowing it was there, without giving it a second thought. Like death, I thought. Like all of this.

The tires hummed on the wet metal bridge and the van shook in sudden gusts of wind and the rain made the sky so dark it felt like nighttime; my mind began to wander. To what we'd find at Mads's, to where Lia was, to how long it would take for Joan to have the cops after me, to how long it would take them to find me. Leaving the phone behind would slow down the process—they couldn't track my cell if it wasn't on and wasn't moving—and perhaps a probation violation wouldn't get them too excited, so I might have a little time. Several hours, a dozen, a day at most. Which was probably all the time we had to find Lia anyway, before she'd been so chopped up that putting her back together would be impossible, or spirited so far away that we'd never track her down, unless by some miracle she was still in one of Mads's freezers, not yet having begun her second life.

And the body's second life, a type of reincarnation, made me remember Dr. Weaver, whose very first words to me, years before, had been, *Do you believe in reincarnation?*

What? I'd said, surprised. The second surprise, as the first had been walking into the operating room I'd just sterilized and finding a doctor I didn't know and hadn't expected, his ungloved hands resting on the body I'd just prepped. I wasn't happy to see him, as now I'd have to start the process all over again, which was both time-consuming and expensive. Taking down the sterile drapes, re-spraying everything with bleach spray, hanging new drapes, moving the body to clean the table once more, washing bacteria from the body yet again. New scrubs, new gloves, everything I thought of meant more money, on top of which it would also be tiring, and I was already tired; it had been three AM, after all.

A surgeon, I guessed. They were famous for caring little about how their behaviors affected others, and sometimes when they saw a familiar name on the dead patient list they came down to cut them open, to see how surgical procedures they'd performed years before had held up over time.

Reincarnation, he said. Do you believe in it?

Well, no, I said. Not in the Buddhist sense.

The Buddhist sense?

Yeah, you know. That you come back as different things depending on how you behave in one life, until you finally achieve enlightenment.

He looked at me for the first time, his turn to appear surprised. I'd never heard that, he said. I was thinking of, you know, coming back as another person.

Well, you probably didn't have time to study world religions in med school.

He shook his head and dropped his hands. So how does it work?

Well, it's not all laid out, I said. I mean, it's not exactly determined what happens. If you're a mean truffle pig, you don't necessarily come back as a truffle.

Not much chance for improvement, though, if you're a truffle.

Probably not, I said. I don't know. Maybe it's just that you're supposed to learn, so that on the next go-round, whatever you are, you'll do better. Even as a pig.

Or as a truffle, he said. I like them, by the way.

Truffles?

Yeah.

Me too.

You've had them?

I was used to surgeons' snobbishness and had long since determined not to let it get under my skin. Part of the point of it, probably, to make you feel their superiority, so why give them that satisfaction?

What about her? he said.

I have no idea if she ever had truffles.

Sorry. Not what I meant, he said, and laid his pale hands once more on the dark arm of the cadaver, a woman in her midtwenties who'd died in surgery. What about Delondre here? he said. What will she come back as?

That he knew her name surprised me. Is she a relative? I said.

No. Someone I was operating on.

I don't know, I said. Maybe she'll be someone who gets to live longer.

That would be nice, he said, and nodded. That would seem fair. She had an aneurysm.

I know, I said. I read the chart. *Always read the chart.* The first thing Dr. Giorgio had taught me. *That way there won't be any big surprises.* If only.

She didn't have to die though, he said, and I thought he was going to admit to a surgical mistake. Some surgeons came by to apologize to patients' bodies they'd been working on, but that turned out not to be the case here.

She gave up, he said. And I was so close. He looked at me with sudden intensity. It happens sometimes. I've got someone open and I'm doing my stuff and my hands are deep inside them and all of the sudden I feel something . . . *let go,* and a few minutes later they die. It happened with her, and she'd almost made it. I wish she'd fought just a little longer, long enough for me to finish.

It was extraordinary. I'd never heard anything like it. Surgeons had near-universal reputations as pricks—even surgical residents hated them—but he seemed to be the exception. I wanted to say something to help him. I looked at the list of what I was to harvest, the things I had permission for, the things I didn't, and chose the former.

You know, she'll get a chance to live on. I'm going to harvest her iliac crest, her pericardial sac, both of her incuses. She'll change lives. People will hear because of her, their hearts will work better. They'll walk.

Yeah, yeah, I know, the wonderful world of transplants, he said, and waved it off. I wanted her to leave the hospital alive and walking. He shook his head again, sighed. What a waste. He leaned over the body and said, You should have fought more, then turned and asked me out.

What? I said, surprised once again. You mean, like on a date?

Yeah, he said. I'd like to take you out. Dinner and a movie maybe. Or we could just put together a picnic and drive along the river to a park. Something with truffles, if we can find them in this godforsaken town.

Why? I couldn't help asking.

For the first time, he smiled. Never had anyone say *that* to me before.

Sorry, I said. I guess I'm just surprised.

Here's why. I don't get a lot of time off and I don't interact with many people because I'm so busy, and most of the other nurses I work with aren't very smart. I don't think a single one of them would have known that about the Buddhists, let alone truffle pigs. They can be hard to talk to, which frankly is a real bummer.

I'm not a nurse, I said. I'm just a procurer.

Wow, he said. You're really trying to figure out novel ways to say no.

It was my turn to smile, and I felt my shoulders drop, my defenses letting down. No, I said. It's just that I didn't want to start things under false pretenses.

Okay, he said. So I'm a surgeon, and you're a procurer, and now that we've got that out of the way, was that a yes?

Yes, I said, and laughed. Which frankly felt a little odd given where we were.

We'd exchanged names and numbers, and he'd promised to call in three days, when he would finally have a bit of free time.

My schedule, he said, shaking his head. It can be brutal. Just want you to know that ahead of time.

I told him I'd look forward to it, and after he left I took a few minutes alone with Delondre's body before resterilizing everything. Not too long, since I only had the room for a couple of hours, but it seemed somehow unholy to do otherwise, now that I knew something about her. When I got home later, after I'd frozen all the tissues and sent the serology off to the lab, cleaned the OR again, and resterilized all my instruments, I showered and wrote Dr. Weaver's name and number on a big index card and put it next to the answering machine, to make him call.

Which worked, three days later, though only to leave a message. I've been thinking about this whole reincarnation thing, he said. Could it work that someone could come back as themselves, only older and wiser? That would be great, wouldn't it? In my case, I'd become a tree surgeon. A lot less stressful, and regular sleep! Anyway, sorry I didn't get to talk to you. Surgery schedule is awful this week. But Friday night might be clear. Will call Friday AM to firm it up!

Friday was six days away. In order not to get my hopes up, I replayed the message only once a day, but when he called back again it was to tell me he'd made dinner reservations at Jack Fry's—my favorite place in the city because of the shrimp and grits, the warm brie salad, the walls covered with photos of historic Louisville, the floods, the Ali fights, the burning yellow school buses during busing riots. The dinner had been spectacular, the after-dinner sex even better. And the two dates after that were glorious, a baseball game and an overnight trip to Chicago, where he'd told me all about feeling like he lived perpetually in his father's shadow, that the old man could just do everything better.

Christ, he'd said, when he'd been unable to take a nap after we'd been to the Navy Pier. My old man can take one any time. How many things can I compete with that guy at? Everything, he supposed. Everything was a competition. Part of the fucking journey, I guess, he'd said.

I was going to help with that, but before I got the chance to, before we even had our fourth date, the story about stolen body parts broke, and on the message he left that time, he said that he was just too busy right then and wished me luck.

I never bothered calling back—what would have been the point?—and now, he either no longer recognized me or pretended not to. Even if I couldn't blame him, I still did;

he'd known the real me, so it wasn't fair of him to bail so easily. Yet once this whole thing with Lia came to light, he'd probably shudder, realizing that, once again, he'd come in contact with a lower form of life.

So be it, I thought. If I was going to be vermin in the eyes of the normal, at least I'd be good at it.

I slapped Amed's shoulder. Faster, I said. I want to get there.

12

Amed gripped and regripped the steering wheel, checked his mirrors repeatedly, glanced my way as often as he dared; I ignored him and looked out the window through the lessening rain, remembering the many times I'd driven deep into Southern Indiana in search of bodies, times I needed to make my quota. Remembering too how the length of the trip had had an inverse correlation to how careful I was as I worked.

Wherever I harvested, I took from the dead to make others' lives better and myself richer, but in southern Indiana, I sometimes sent the dead off with mementos of me as well. At times I had good reasons—wooden dowels, say, left in place of plundered leg bones so that pants would still fit properly and open casket viewers wouldn't be shocked—but most often it was a question of speed, so that I left mosquito hemostats or bone wax, umbilical tape, deavers or retractors, pencil cauteries, suction tips, and sponges inside a harvested body as I hurriedly sewed it up to hide my passage. Part of the business, but I couldn't help reflecting now that it became more and more frequent the longer I'd been at it.

Near the farming town of Duncan we passed a group of migrant laborers picking corn, the corn torn and battered from the storms as if a madman had driven a truck through the fields, and I remembered my boss Kevin pointing out laborers years before, harvesting strawberries near these very fields. He'd said, Those Mexicans? They're us.

How do you know they're Mexicans?

He frowned. You know what I mean. Migrant labor in a foreign country, the ones no one pays any attention to or wants to know about. That's what we are, with corpses. Migrants in the land of the dead.

Well, I said, unlike them we'll all end up citizens.

Yeah, and isn't that a bonus? he said. But seriously. If things go wrong, they're the ones who pay. Same in our field. It's not the surgical suppliers that ever have problems. It's us. Scandals stop with the low guys. Watch. You'll see.

Later, after the story broke and everything had fallen apart, after CGI had left me to fend for myself, I'd tried to contact him, to tell him he should have gone into fortune-telling, only to discover that his fortune-telling abilities didn't apply to himself; he'd ended up in prison for a dozen years.

Are you not going to talk to me at all? Amed said.

In response I turned on the radio, which, to my surprise, was tuned to a country and western station. As the landscape became increasingly steep and piney, I said, I used to come this way to buy Christmas trees, the memory popping from my mouth before I could stifle it.

As a kid? Amed said.

As a teen, I said. As a kid I lived up north.

Yeah, he said. That's right. You have that look about you.

What look?

An immigrant.

Takes one to know one, I said.

He shook his head. Not me. My parents are immigrants. Born here. Raised too. Shepherd's Square.

Tough neighborhood, I said, and it was, home to the city's deadliest projects. Another fertile recruiting ground, back in the day. I asked, How'd you become a chef from there?

Long story.

I got the sense he wanted me to ask, but I didn't, not after what he'd done to Lia, which I couldn't forgive. But I didn't want to be silent anymore either, so I asked what year his parents had immigrated.

1985.

Everyone in the body trade knew that year, the year the Indian government outlawed the trading of human parts after a huge scandal—the bodies of eight hundred Buddhist monks plundered by Indian wranglers. That had changed everything, setting off a mad scramble for what had once been a reliable commodity, and giving rise to people like me, since for decades India had supplied most of the world's bones.

Were your parents in the business? I asked.

They were, he said.

So it was easy for you to pick it up. Christ, I said. I should have seen that one coming.

After we stopped and started twice, the traffic accordianing slowly forward—backed up because of downed trees and power lines from the recent storm and the crews working on them—he pulled over and said, I think I'm going to be sick.

He opened the door and leaned out and threw up. Lia had been able to throw up at will, in order to get out of bad dates, so I said nothing, expecting that he would say now that we shouldn't go on.

Listen, he said. This is a mistake. We really shouldn't be doing this. I didn't tell you everything about Mads.

Let me guess. He has two heads, right?

He told me to kill your cat.

Stop, I said. I don't believe you. And I didn't, even though my breathing had begun to grow shallow, even though he looked deathly. He'd lied about everything else, so why not this? When was that? I asked.

When I was at your house.

You told him you were there? Was that his plan too?

Of course not. We took the body and then you showed up and started asking questions and he got nervous. I texted him that the whole thing was crazy. That you didn't know anything, that you weren't going to be a problem. He told me to be sure. He told me to kill the cat.

Just shut up and drive, I said.

Elena, please. I'm begging you. This won't end well.

I ignored him, grabbing his phone off the dashboard, deleting each of his contacts. His phone would be as empty as mine, because I'd lost most of my friends before the trial and almost all of the rest after. Perhaps Lia had turned them away from me, though that wasn't really fair; many would have left on their own and the rest I never bothered recontacting, even if they called me. Too much to explain. And easier to not always have to be reminded by looks or conversational ellipses.

* * *

Ten miles from Corydon we circled down a long exit ramp and came out near an old collapsed barn that I remembered from our Christmas tree days, before my mother had moved back north, before she'd died. Each year it had buckled a bit more and now it was completely gone, a tangle of wood and brambles.

Despite my earlier bravado, I was growing afraid. What if Mads was as bad as Belmont and Amed said? Well, it was too late to back out now. I tried to control my breathing and concentrated on the passing landscape, farmland with rolled green hay in the fields, dropped like slices from a massive round loaf, a preserve for orphaned deer, small ranch houses on big lots with signs at the ends of the driveway, advertising firewood for sale or small engine repair or massage services. A couple of trailer parks, one horribly forlorn, the other a mile farther and more homey, with boxwood and peonies and flags, a large, aboveground pool. Empty gas stations, a big lot selling tractors and combines, its multicolored pennants whipping in the wind, smaller lots selling used cars, and now and then a new mansion, high up on a hill far back from the road, natives who'd made it big elsewhere and returned home. Trees, beginning to retake abandoned fields.

At the next intersection the sign for Corydon pointed left, and we turned right; I was just as glad. It was a pretty small town, hanging flower baskets along the leafy town square, where lawyers, banks, and cafés still thrived, but early in my wrangling career the director of the Limeberry Funeral Home had insisted I eat with a donor's family. I eat with the family of everyone I bury, he'd said, and if I wanted to keep working with him, I had to too. It spooked me, and after that trip others from CGI had had to cover that route, as I'd already started cutting corners and I didn't want to do that to someone who trusted me. Business with the dishonest was preferable; it made my own elisions seem less damning.

We turned off the state highway to a smaller road and Amed hit his blinker. Up ahead was a terrible-looking trailer, rust-streaked, one corner crumpled, smack against the road, jumbled dog houses and old bikes and parts of an old car engine piled on its sagging porch.

That place? I said, and felt myself shrink away from the window.

He nodded. Though that's mostly to keep the curious out.

The driveway slipped past the trailer and down into a hollow, winding around an old apple orchard. The green fruit on the trees hung low and bumped against the car. There, he said, as we turned the corner to find three other trailers, newer and laid out in a U shape. INDIANA MEDICAL SUPPLIES was written on a small sign hung from the porch of the middle one.

His truck's here, he said, nodding at the pickup parked under a pin oak, deep blue or black or forest green, it was hard to tell in the gloomy, post-storm light.

Are you kidding? I said when I saw its bumper sticker: I HEART WATERBOARDING.

When I reached for the car door Amed grabbed my arm and said, Wait.

I was about to tell him to let go when a barking rott-weiler rushed from around the far trailer and bulleted toward us, teeth bared, back fur up, tail low and pointed.

Christ, I said, jerking away from the door as the dog slammed into it, claws and teeth scrabbling at the window, leaving a trail of saliva. Why didn't you tell me?

You didn't give me a chance. He reached behind the seat for a pair of flip-flops. You'll need these, he said. He dropped them on my lap, climbed out, and ripped open a Slim Jim and said, Butch, here, and tossed it over the car, away from the trailer.

Butch immediately turned after the Slim Jim.

Okay, Amed said, leaning into the car. Now's our chance. Better hurry. Then he turned and sprinted toward the central trailer.

He threw the door open and went in as it banged against the wall, which I thought foolish, since people in southern Indiana were famous for using guns on people who arrived unannounced (I'd collected a lot of bodies who'd been shot trespassing, or robbing, or by mistake) but Butch was almost done with the Slim Jim and Amed was still standing and I decided I'd take my chances, so I slipped the flip-flops on over my bruised soles and told myself to run, gauging the fifteen massive yards, the gravel as sharp as spikes through the flip-flops, my legs pumping, my head thrown back as I took in huge gulps of air.

Butch was running too, gaining on me, his breathing louder than mine, his legs unfairly long. I didn't look back, knowing I'd fall if I did, screaming a prayer in my head, *Please, let me make it.* His paws crunched over the gravel at my heels.

Safe! I thought as I burst across the threshold and Amed slammed the door behind me, Butch thundering against it, growling and barking in his fury. And then a big, bearded guy in dirty scrubs holding a scalpel stepped into the next doorway. The air smelled of warming meat.

I told you never to bring anybody here unless they were dead, he said, in a voice so gravelly it seemed to come from the bottom of a mine. He glared at me with his tiny blue eyes and shifted the scalpel from his left hand to his right.

Oh no, I thought. *Oh fuck.*

Amed shuffled closer over the shiny floor, standing between me and the door. *He's breathing too fast*, I thought.

I had to, he said, pushing my shoulder, pushing me forward. I had to. She knew about the body.

13

The power was out, the room baking. I smelled sweat—mine, Amed's, Mads's—and wondered if that was to be the last thing I ever noticed. Whatever they had planned for me was going to happen; I was merely a bystander, perhaps a sacrificial one.

We stood like that for seconds, Butch still barking madly outside. Mads was so large he filled the doorway. Dirty curly blond hair, dirtier blond bushy beard, a big round face and camo scrubs that barely stretched over his huge arms. He seemed to be reddening as he watched me, like a Viking being boiled from within.

Mads stepped toward me and I remembered Amed's words: *I'm good with a knife*, he'd said, and: *You could leave this place and no one would ever notice*, and lost control of my bladder, the scent of urine overlaying those of sweat and meat.

Mads stopped, his head moving back a notch. What the fuck is wrong with her? he said. She just peed her pants. Jesus, he said, sounding like an old-school preacher beseeching the lord. Did you bring someone with the plague? She looks like she's dying.

Which relieved me, because if he was talking about me dying, he probably didn't plan to kill me.

Amed said, Sorry, Mads. She said she'd call the cops if we didn't come.

Mads lowered the scalpel. So what? Everything I do is legal.

That's not true, I said, beginning to feel combative again. I know what's legal.

Yeah, that's right, Mads said. Amed told me you're the industry poster child.

I *was*. Always room for a new one.

He shook his head. Not going to happen. From what Amed told me, I could cut you up and sell you off and no one would bother looking for you. And quite a happy crowd, if they did ever find out.

It spooked me, but it didn't scare me into silence; he'd missed his chance somehow. No, I said. Probably not. Not the kind of people you mean. Friends, family. But the cops are already looking for me. Probation violation.

He sucked his teeth and said, Well, that's okay. You didn't drive your car and you probably didn't tell anyone where you went. They can look all they want, since they won't be looking here. My advice is to get back into Amed's van and go before you wish you'd never come.

No, I said, shaking my head. Not until I know what you did with my friend.

Cindy Lownes? he said.

Come on, Amed said. You know that's not her name.

I was glad he'd taken my side. Until then I wasn't sure what he'd do, and now I was certain he hadn't brought me here to bury me.

No, Mads said, the paperwork lists Cindy Lownes. I filed it in triplicate. Got the death certificate, the coroner's report, the family's permission to harvest. He checked his steel wristwatch, so big it looked like it came from a clock tower. I filed it all days ago, he said.

That's bullshit, Amed said. Forged, and you know it.

How would I know that? he said, his voice growing deeper, as if he'd shoveled in more gravel. I depend on the good faith of the people I work with. Which in this case is you. So if there's a crime here, I'm not the one who committed it.

I took a half-step toward him. Mads, we don't want trouble.

Then you shouldn't have come. I already told you that. He rolled the scalpel over in his hand and then again, swiftly, and said, And I don't want to tell you twice.

I know, I said, uncomfortable in my soaked pants. All I need to know is where Lia went. I'll explain the mix-up. I just want to bring her home. Her mother, you know? She's devastated.

He seemed to be thinking it over and then he smiled, which was worse; his teeth were crooked and stained.

Let me get this straight. You want me to tell you where I shipped a corpse I was legally entitled to, and which right now is being used in a surgical conference, so you two can go and screw up a contract I spent two years getting. A contract that's worth one and a half million dollars. Does that sound about right?

Mads, Amed said. It's one body. They'll understand.

They will, will they? And you know this how? You've dealt with these people? Built up a relationship with them over years, never missed a deadline, never not filled an order, worked like a dog day and night to be sure they were satisfied? It's your reputation you're putting on the line?

People make mistakes, Amed said.

Yeah, and the biggest one I've seen in years is the two of you, standing here. Now get the fuck out.

I wasn't sure what would happen next until Mads's phone rang on the table beside us. Amed reached for it.

Don't touch that, Mads said, and stepped to pick it up.

I fought the powerful urge to kick him in the balls.

He looked at the number and flicked the phone open and said, What?

Above his beard, his face grew redder as he listened. Fuck, he said. He listened some more and said, No, I don't have enough ice to fix that problem, and besides, it would be melted by the time I got there. So fix it yourself.

He shut the phone off and tossed it down.

Listen, Mads, I said. I've got a problem.

No shit, he said. We've been over it. Now get out.

Not that, this, I said, and pointed to my stained pants.

Can you please let me change before we go? I don't want to ride like this.

He laughed. I don't have any clothes for you. So unless you brought any with you, you're shit out of luck.

Amed's got spare clothes in his van.

All right, Mads said, and nodded. Get her something, but be quick about it.

Amed said, I'm not going out there with Butch on the prowl.

Yeah, you will, Mads said. Either that or your van can smell like piss the whole way back to Louisville.

Please, Mads? I said. You got what you wanted. We're leaving. Can't you call the dog off?

He sighed. You're a real ball-buster, you know that? No wonder Belmont worried about you.

I didn't mind the insult; it meant he'd do as I asked. I shuffled closer to the table to let him by.

He opened the door and called out to Butch, Amed watching over his shoulder. While they had their backs turned I clicked the phone to life and thumbed to recent calls. French Lick Springs Resort. I'd turned it off and stepped away by the time Mads had Butch by the collar.

* * *

In the bathroom, I cleaned myself up and scribbled a note and tucked it into the pocket of the pants I left behind, in case Mads's acquiescence was just an act. *Elena Kelly was alive here. Check his brother's crematorium.* When I came out, the two of them were by the table, Mads gripping the scalpel in one hand and Butch's collar in the other. Muscles tensed under his smooth brown skin, Butch looked ready to spring.

Thanks, I said.

Mads's phone rang again and Amed reached for it and Mads slammed the scalpel down through Amed's hand, pinning it to the table.

At first, Amed looked calmly at his pierced hand, as if nothing had happened. Then he howled in pain and Butch began barking.

I told you not to touch my stuff, Mads said. He picked up the phone and walked to the door and answered it, leaving Amed impaled, his face draining of color.

I yanked the scalpel out and pressed my hand on the wound and raised Amed's arm above his head and tugged him toward the bathroom, where there'd been a first-aid kit bolted to the wall. I'd noticed it because of the bumper sticker pasted across it. AGAINST THEIR WILL AND WITHOUT THEIR KNOWLEDGE.

It's all right, I said, trying to calm him down, since he was beginning to hyperventilate. You'll be okay, I said, and pushed his hand under the water. Hold it there, I said, and opened the first-aid kit.

He stared at the blood running down his fingers and threading through the water while I opened a sterile dressing and squeezed antibiotic cream on it, worried about that scalpel. The smell of decay meant that Mads had been working on a body when we arrived; Amed was probably thinking the same thing.

Here, I said, and handed him some soap. Scrub it quickly.

Then I handed him some balled-up gauze. After he dried it he flattened his hand on the counter. I pressed a dressing to the front and back of his palm and taped them in place and raised his arm again. Come on, I said, let's go.

Mads wasn't in the next room or on the porch or anywhere else we could see, but his voice, raised and angry and sepulchral-sounding in the muggy air, came from around the far corner, as if he were some kind of furious announcer in the land of the dead. Move, I said, and tugged Amed to the passenger side of the van and dragged his seatbelt across his shoulder and snapped him in and then hurried around to the driver's side just as Butch sprinted barking around the corner, teeth bared and ears laid flat along his muscular brown head. Our going-away present from Mads, who stood watching us now from the edge of the drive.

I didn't hear what he shouted as I sped off, though the rock he hurled at us clanged loudly off the van, and Butch accompanied us all the way to road, barking and leaping at my window even after I swerved and tried to throw him off.

Fuck, Amed said, rocking as I bumped up onto the pavement. He held his hand up and inspected the bloody mess. Harrison County Hospital is ten miles, he said.

We're not going there, I said.

What? he said, and waved his hand. I have to get this taken care of.

We will, I said, in French Lick.

Screw that. That's forty-five minutes away.

Lia's in French Lick.

189

How do you know that?

The phone call he got was from there. The resort. You heard what he said. Bodies are decomposing. They must be without power too. Which means it's some kind of surgical conference.

Doesn't mean they're using Lia's body.

No, you're right, I said, as we came to an intersection. Without stopping I turned north. But it's our best shot, and I'm not going to miss it.

I'm bleeding, he said. Drop me off first.

When I didn't stop, he said, This is going to go wrong. Once Mads finds out, it's bound to.

He won't find out, I said. Not in time. *And by then*, I thought, *I'll be in prison.*

14

The drive to French Lick reminded me of Lia's old joke: *Why do birds fly upside down over Indiana? Because there's nothing worth shitting on in the entire state.* The countryside was pretty—fifteen miles of a piney state forest, which retreated from the roadway here and there to reveal corn growing up the green hills, yellow and tasseled at its tips, or the huge Lake Pakota surrounding stretches of both sides of the road with choppy whitecaps—but beauty didn't bring jobs, and I'd wrangled quite a few corpses from the area, many young, most dead from meth, guns, or accidents. Nearly every mile marker sported a dead deer—how much easier it would have been if we could have wrangled *those*—and every third or fourth featured some barefoot teenage boy speeding along the shoulder on an ATV, an oversized gas can strapped to its body. Human bombs; every summer, five or six died that way in the surrounding counties.

Boaters were getting off the lake and loading their boats onto trailers, which they towed behind their pickups at a crawling rate up the long steep hills. Impatient and reckless, other drivers pulled out to pass on the two-lane highway, even as the onrushing approaching cars honked and flashed their headlights.

We entered the semidecrepit resort town of French Lick slowly, winding around trees downed in the storms outside the Wendy's and on the long, once-stately approach and circular drive outside the casino entrance, where we avoided people gathered in little knots, staring up at its magnificently massive yellow-brick façade. They talked excitedly, as if there were a fire. Not a fire, but a power outage of long duration, which meant that the air-conditioning was no longer working, which in turn meant that the bodies in the surgical conference were beginning to smell. The odor was escaping from doors and vents into other parts of the hotel, including wedding receptions in the adjoining ballrooms.

One bride sobbed on the violet-clad shoulders of two bridesmaids, but the other, tomato-faced in anger, stood on perilous heels berating a manager in a shiny beige suit.

Jesus, Amed said, rallying as we made our way through the buzzing crowd. What a mess.

It was—people so upset I was almost surprised no one had gone down the road to Freckles Guns and come back shooting—but I tugged him after me and said, No, an opportunity. The bodies need to be moved.

The surgical conference was in Windsor II, so we headed across the vaulted, gilded lobby to the event section, where even the high-ceilinged hallways were grand affairs, chande-liered, wood-paneled and lushly carpeted, spacious enough to fit a train. Every few feet along the soft path were sign-boards—Breast Augmentation and Reconstruction—with bright blue arrows pointing ahead. On the way up, I'd searched for conference information on Amed's phone.

Wait, Amed kept saying. What are we going to do?

Already we were at the door. The wrangler—a flushed, unhappy face, sweat crescents arcing beneath each arm of his green button-down shirt—was explaining to an irate older man in a morning suit that the power outage wasn't his fault.

Sir, he said, and shook his head. None of us *planned* this.

You didn't plan the conference?

Of course we did. But we didn't plan for the power to go out.

Well it has, and the smell of these bodies is awful. What on earth made you think having it next door to a wedding reception was a good idea in the first place?

Excuse me, I said, and slipped between them. Mads sent us, I said. We're supposed to help you out.

Jesus, the wrangler said, relieved. I thought he wasn't going to do a thing.

He's a better businessman than that, I said, and swiveled to the elderly gentleman. Sir, I said. I'm terribly sorry about this. My advice is to go back to your wedding party and tell them that, within half an hour, all of this will be cleared up.

He wasn't done—he started to repeat his protests to me—but I held up my hand and said sternly, Sir, I know you're angry. I would be too. But right now isn't the time for satisfaction. That will come later, in court. Now's the time to fix things.

Already I was moving beyond them, toward the bodies laid out on the tables, six women, faces and torsos shrouded, three of the cadavers' newly enhanced breasts pointing at the ceiling. I turned down the sheet on the first one and the next and the next, hardly pausing to look, and then all of the second row and stood staring at the pale face of the last, barely able to breathe.

Is that her? Amed said, standing beside me.

I smoothed her brunette hair. No, I said. None of them are.

It seemed impossible. I'd come all this way, certain that I'd find her, that I'd bring Mrs. Stefanini some peace. I'd been prepared for it, I thought, ready to look upon the dead face of the person I held dearest in all the world, but I realized now, gazing at the unmoving features and damp skin of a stranger, that I hadn't been prepared, that uncovering Lia would have dropped me to my knees with howls of grief. Yet even so *not* seeing her, *not* finding her, was worse. It was as if she'd been wiped from the surface of the earth, as if I'd been sent on this scavenger hunt as a way to increase my pain rather than assuage it, as if my past sins were going to haunt me forever; Mrs. Stefanini had turned to me as a last resort and again I'd failed her.

I covered the corpse's face, and as the sheet settled over her features I had the odd sensation that it *was* Lia, that I simply hadn't been ready to admit it, so I yanked the sheet

back and once more was confronted with a stranger. I left
her uncovered and turned away.

The wrangler said, You're going to take all of them?

No, I said, no, we can't take them all, and I shouldered
beyond him. We can't.

You have to, he said, maneuvering again to block my
way. Christ. I've got six more in the back, and the hotel will
have my balls if I don't move them *now*.

I grabbed a handful of his sweaty shirt. Six more in the
back? I said. Where?

He talked the whole way there, though he might as
well have been a bluebird for all I understood him. The six
were in the back hallway, one next to the other, covered in
white muslin like bizarrely large loaves of bread, awaiting
their turn in the oven. I turned back the face shrouds of
the first five one after the other, but none of them was Lia.
On the last one I rested my hand on the exposed shoulder
and thought, *It's all right, it's her,* and didn't turn down
the sheet.

This one, I said. We'll start with her.

But why? the wrangler said. The others in the hotel are
much worse. Everyone's *seen* those.

Yes, I said. Exactly. So we'll take these out the service
entrance, one at a time, and while we do that you'll begin
ferrying the others this way. The crowd's already angry.
You want them after us while we're handling bodies?

I don't think I've ever seen someone look more grateful, and as soon as he left Amed said, We can't take all of
them. Not a chance.

We won't. Just this one, I said, patting the last corpse. It's her.

You haven't even looked.

I will. Now get the van.

But what about the others? You going to leave this guy stuck with them?

He was stuck with them anyway. What happens after isn't our concern.

That's crazy. Mads will kill us when he hears about this. He'll find us.

Yes, probably. But not right away. Not before we bring her back. And I suspect that by that time he'll have other problems to deal with. Now go, Amed.

After his footsteps had faded away down the hallway, after the service door banged open, I slid between the last two gurneys and cut the final corpse from the herd, walking it toward the exit. Once there, I stood for a long time, one hand resting on the warming flesh of her truncated shin; her feet and ankles had all been cut off, probably sent to some podiatry conference. I pretended that she was alive, that we were somewhere we'd both liked—a concert, the beach, the tobacco barns—and had been dancing or swimming or running and now we were sweaty and winded, happy to be together, to be alive. It was the only way I could keep from dissolving.

Once I heard the van backing up outside, I opened the service door and directed Amed to keep backing up by hand signals through the rear window. I had both cargo doors open before he was out.

No body bag? he said.

We don't have time for it. Hurry, I said. He'll be back soon.

As if on cue, I heard the wrangler pushing the next gurney down the hall. Then he stopped and raised voices reached us.

Amed and I didn't wait; we lifted the body and swiftly loaded it and hurried to our seats and headed out.

I wasn't sure—the engine was old, the transmission noisy—but I thought someone was running behind us and shouting, though I never saw anyone in my side-view mirror.

* * *

Soon we were clear of the town and joining a steady stream of traffic heading south and east. For a long time Amed said nothing, but after ten miles or so, when we'd passed the last of the downed trees from the storm and the long line of traffic had begun to stretch out on the causeway crossing Lake Pakota, he said, How come you never looked? It might not even be her. Then we'd have Mads after us for nothing.

It's her, I said.

You recognized her shoulder? Or you looked when I was getting the van?

Neither, I said. It's her.

I glanced out the window at the turbulent water so he wouldn't see my overflowing eyes. Her hand had slipped free of the sheet as we moved her, her wrist, her forearm. Belmont had been wrong. The scar was still there, as big as a sand dollar, shiny and smooth and slightly raised, evidence of her ongoing attempts to erase me from her life. The bitter irony was that she'd wanted nothing to do with me, all the way to the end.

15

Are you sure? I asked Amed as we pulled into the Harrison County Hospital. Why not just let me take you across the river to Louisville?

We were near Corydon, land of caves and covered bridges, small-town America at its best—July sweet corn celebrations, October apple festivals, December Christmas fairs, sturdy stone and stately brick buildings surrounding its still-vibrant town square—the kind of place where all three thousand residents would profess shock at the work I'd done. Except that I'd driven the twenty-five miles from Louisville to Corydon often in my wrangling years, to collect bodies or their parts from its hospital and funeral parlors, its doctors and undertakers, as the dead weren't any safer in benign small-town America than in the predatory big cities.

I don't want any record of my hospitalization, Amed said. I'll say a screwdriver slipped, but they might be suspicious.

You think? Doesn't look like a screwdriver wound.

Right. So, if there's a police report, I don't want it cir-
culating in Louisville.

I didn't think police reports stopped at the river, but I
was too tired to get into it with him. I'd have to go to the
police after I dropped Lia at the funeral home anyway, and
once I did, Amed would have a lot of other questions to answer. I almost felt bad for him, considering that he'd helped
me recover Lia. Almost.

All right, I said. I'll let you out here then. How will you
get home?

Greyhound. I'll be fine.

He reached into his front pocket for his phone. Here.
Take this. I'll text you when I'm back at my apartment.
You can bring the van by.

If I've got your phone, how'll you text me?

Yours is back at my apartment, remember?

Right, I said, and nodded.

He got out and stood on the pavement, looking as if he
was about to say something important, which I didn't want
to hear. I put the van in gear and said, Better shut the door.

Elena, he said. Where are you taking her?

Hapsburg Funeral Home. Her father was laid out there,
so I guess that's the family place.

Good, he said and blinked repeatedly. If the guy gives
you any trouble? Hapsburg's not what he seems. I've
worked with him plenty of times. He sold me Lia's boots.

The bastard, I thought. *The sanctimonious lying bastard.*

* * *

When I left the hospital parking lot, I drove south and west, away from 64, certain that the wrangler at French Lick would have called Mads. And, knowing I'd head back to Louisville, Mads would be looking for me on 64, waiting somewhere before the Sherman Minton Bridge. But I could cross the Ohio farther south by Mauckport—famous in the wrangling field for the 1974 day when half the town died in a single tornado. Soon I'd left the Corydon hills and was surrounded by flat acres of corn, withered by summer drought, muddy from recent rains. I should have known where I was going, guided by my past, but for miles nothing looked familiar, and when I turned around and tried to make my way back to Corydon I must have missed a fork, because soon I was hopelessly lost. I stopped, hesitated, and then decided to keep heading southwest, toward the Ohio River and Kentucky.

I knew I was near the river when I drove through a sudden gust of fog, and when I rolled my window down for air, thinking it would keep me awake, I smelled its muddy scent. Then the fog thickened, obscuring the road, and I slowed and flicked on the lights, worried someone would rear-end me. Wouldn't that be a perfect end to my day, explaining to a cop what I was doing with a body, one missing its feet and ankles.

I crawled along with my window open for what seemed like miles, the chilly fog swirling into the van. Not a single car passed and I began to feel that I was stuck in place, that

I was going to stay lost in this fog forever, which spooked me. I knew I was tired, that I was overreacting, but I couldn't stop myself as I stepped on the accelerator and sped faster and faster. Yet even then I felt like I wasn't moving, that in entering the fog I'd descended into a dream underworld where the engine was on but the transmission not engaged, where I could watch one peculiar image after another appear to me out of the onrushing mist, where I could do nothing but hallucinate and dream. So I dreamed that I was dreaming and then I was, that Dr. Handler told me that her shadow had always been female, even when she was a young boy, that a blue golf cart was making its slow way down the road before me pulled by a palomino horse, that the horse was Lia and I had to swerve to avoid her. I did, then woke to the sound of crashing and slammed on my brakes and screamed.

The sudden quiet startled me. There had been no shattering glass, no tearing metal, and as I checked my face and hands, patted my upper body, I realized I was unhurt, so I pushed open the door and stepped out and stumbled back down the van, my feet tangled in crackling stubble. As if on cue, the fog began to clear and, leading from the road where it had swerved left and I had gone straight, was a short plowed patch of ruined corn.

Jesus, I said aloud. You were lucky.

That turned out to be not quite the case. Though the van wasn't damaged, aside from fresh scratches in the faded paint, and though the engine and transmission still worked, the left rear tire was flat. I sat on the tilted rear bumper, head in my hands, collecting myself, until I heard

Lia's voice in my head, *Nothing to it but to do it.* Which made me smile. So I slapped both thighs, stood up, and opened the van doors in search of a jack. Miraculously, Lia was still covered up, and I shifted her legs aside and some old clothes and towels and found it—another miracle, I decided, since it could just as easily have been the case that Amed had discarded the jack long ago—and worked it free.

But I came to the end of my good luck almost instantly; each time I levered the arm to raise the van the jack sank into the mud. I could crank for hours and end up never getting the van lifted, which made changing the tire impossible. For a few exhausted minutes, I squatted next to the ticking van staring at the jack, and then, worse luck, someone stopped to help me. Worse still, I realized as I looked up at the sounds of a slowing engine and tires crunching over gravel, was that it was Mads.

* * *

My blood seemed to drain to my feet; I felt hollow and couldn't move. He sat in the cab making a call and I realized I wasn't breathing. The police? No. Perhaps the wrangler, letting him know he'd found me. I was alone in a withered cornfield in a deserted corner of Indiana and no one knew I was there. But I made myself breathe. I had the jack handle in my hand and I took another breath and turned it; as soon as he was close enough, I was going to swing. Lia deserved at least a fight. I hadn't protected her during life; I could, would, during death, at least for a little while.

Waiting made it worse. My skin itched, my arms trembled, sweat soaked my back. Did he intend fear to overwhelm me? *Hurry, please,* I thought, and I'd begun walking toward him when something about the truck struck me as off. I stopped and studied it—the same make, the same deep-green color, but the I HEART WATERBOARDING bumper sticker was gone. And the driver, when he at last climbed out, wasn't Mads, but was instead much shorter and more compact. Jim, he said. He had a buzz cut and a mustache as straight as a comb and his handshake stopped just short of being crushing. Right away he peppered me with questions, my name (Julie), where I was headed (Chicago), and why (work).

Those your work clothes? he said.

No, I said, realizing I had on Amed's old pants. I forced a laugh. Those are in the back, I said.

What else you got in there? he said, and made a move to open the rear doors.

Work stuff, I said, stepping in front of him.

He didn't say anything but his eyes were coolly appraising, and I realized he was much smarter than his patter made him sound. At last he took a half step back and said, You work in construction?

No, the medical field, I said. Why?

Oh. I was thinking you might have a board handy. Never mind. I do, and with that he turned and retrieved a long plank from the bed of his pickup. We'll just slip this under the jack and it should keep everything from sinking.

His questions, the truck, I couldn't shake the sense that Mads had sent him, that he was meant to distract and delay me until Mads arrived. And who had he been calling? I couldn't ask without sounding overly suspicious, especially if he was just a Good Samaritan stopping to help me, but every nerve in my body was jangling.

How's Mads? I asked.

Please? he said, and smiled.

Mads? Don't you work for him?

He knelt and put the board in place and shifted the jack onto it and stood. Mads? He said. No. Sorry. You must have me confused with someone else. So, he said conversationally, you done with that jack handle?

I looked down at it in my hand. Once I handed it to him I'd be at his mercy, and the thought terrified me, but I couldn't hold onto it if I wanted him to change the tire, if I had even the smallest belief that he was simply trying to help me. If he wasn't, I decided, it wouldn't much matter; it would all be over soon anyway. Tired and afraid and with my mind running on as if I were drunk, I held it out to him.

Thanks, he said, and took it without seeming to notice that I'd hesitated. He bent to lever the jack, but before he started he turned and said, So, what happened, anyway? How'd you go off the road?

I held up Amed's phone and pretended to be abashed. Lost, I said. Looking at my phone while trying to get directions.

He clucked his tongue. You know, I always tell my wife her phone is going to get her killed. I hope maybe you've learned your lesson. Then, as if to remove the sting from his rebuke, he said, Of course, it's not like I haven't done it once or twice myself, and, to my immense relief, with that he set to it.

The mist burned off and the slanting late-afternoon sun was baking the earth dry, warming my back, heating the van. Cars passed by and I couldn't help but look up at each one, worried it was a cop, terrified it would be Mads, until I noticed Jim watching me once or twice, and after that I concentrated on his work, his arms pumping as he levered the jack, the way he knelt to see if the tire was clear of the mud. If I didn't trust him, I needed him to trust me.

When he had the van sufficiently raised he pulled the handle from the jack, reversed it, and pried off the hubcap to get at the lug nuts.

You're going to get your hands dirty, because I'll need you to hold the tire in place while I do this, he said. You okay with that?

Of course, I said, and stepped to it.

While he worked, Jim told me that he was headed to one of the construction sites to oversee the pouring of a foundation, that he was glad for the excuse to help me because the contractor was always late and he hated waiting for him. Then he loosened the last of the lug nuts and unscrewed it. Was it my imagination, or was he moving ridiculously slowly? I knew my perceptions were off: sleeplessness, fear, adrenaline, but still, this seemed to be taking too long. More and more trucks passed by, too many of them the color of Jim's truck, of Mads's.

I'd forgotten how long this took, I said, which I hoped would spur him.

However he took it, Jim didn't begin to move more quickly. Let's just get the tire, shall we? he said, and pulled it off the back door of the van, which was beginning to smell in the warming air. I resisted the urge to stand beside him, to lean against the door—paranoid that he was curious about just exactly what was inside—and then he had the spare off and rolled it into place.

Putting it on and slapping the flat tire where the spare had been did seem to take less time, and after breaking the jack down and pulling free his board he clapped his hands clean and said, Good as new. Well, he said, squatting and running his hand over the spare, good as a new marble maybe. I wouldn't go too far on that. Balder than a baby's backside. Chicago, you said? I'd stop off in New Albany and buy a new one. Maybe three or four, he said, leaning back to take in the front tire too.

Good idea, Jim, I said. I can't thank you enough. I wanted to be on the move, certain now I'd lingered far too long. I'd like to pay you for your time, but I don't have any cash. Can you give me an address?

He looked offended. Pay me?

It's just that you didn't have to stop, I said.

Oh, yes I did, he said, and smiled. Where I come from, we don't pass people who are stranded. Man or woman, young or old.

He still hadn't stood; he had to be delaying me, I was certain of it.

All right, I said, holding out my hand for him to shake, standing far enough away that he had to stand. Once he did, I was going to get in the van and back out.

You're welcome, he said. Think nothing of it. But I

have to ask, he said, still holding onto my hand as he tilted his head back and breathed in deeply through his nose, What *is* that smell? You got a deer in there?

Now I was certain he worked for Mads, that he'd known what was in the van all along and had been sent to keep me here until Mads arrived. But I had to play along. If he suspected I knew, he'd keep me from leaving.

Yes, I said, and barked a laugh. My family misses venison up in Chicago. When that didn't seem to work, I laughed again and tented my blouse away from my skin. Me, I'm afraid. That smell. Sweating like a pig. Sorry. It was hard work trying to change that tire before you came.

Uh huh, he said, plainly not believing me. He raised his eyebrows and waited for me to say something else, but I outwaited him, keeping my gaze steady on his puzzled face until at last he let out a long sigh.

Well, all the better I did then, he said. I'll just stay here and make sure you get out. Normally, I'd suggest you go tell the farmer whose field this was, if the corn had any chance of being harvested. But it's all dead. He checked his wristwatch—which was as big as Mads's—and said, He was just going to plow it back under anyway, probably, so all you did is save him some work.

He was as good as his word, driving off once I was back on the shoulder, which shocked me, and I sat for a few moments watching his truck disappear behind a curving line of pines. I couldn't tell if I'd been wrong about him. I hadn't expected him to let me get in the van or for him to drive off, and now I wondered if it was all a trick, if Mads was waiting for me around the corner. Or if Jim was turning around to follow me even as I waited.

I lowered my face to my hands, which smelled now of dirt and rubber, murmuring, *Too close too close too close. Too close by far.* I couldn't let anything like that happen again so I turned the van around and headed back in the other direction, and when I rounded the bend and found no one waiting—no one even on the road and no one in my rearview mirror—I stomped on the accelerator and gripped the wheel. Nothing was going to stop me now.

* * *

Except my bladder. Two miles later, groin burning, I pulled into the first gas station I saw, where I bought a cup of coffee and a toothbrush and toothpaste and took my purchases to the restroom.

My mirrored reflection was shocking—dirt-streaked face, baggy eyes, matted hair. I smelled too, which made it surprising that the woman behind the counter hadn't said anything. I set the coffee on the paper towel dispenser and went to the bathroom and scrubbed my face and hands and ran my damp fingers through my hair, fluffing it and combing it roughly into place, and shook my head when I was done, vigorously. Which helped a little. And though I never liked to brush my teeth before having coffee I made an exception, so that when I stepped out of the bathroom I was feeling semihuman again. I held the coffee to my nose and inhaled. Vanilla and burned sugar; the aroma jolted me awake.

Maybe getting a flat tire wasn't such a bad thing after all, I told myself, feeling better, feeling lucky for the first time in days, but when I came out of the store I dropped my coffee and my stomach clenched. Jim stood by the back of Amed's van, staring into the open back door.

16

What are you doing? I asked. When he turned to face me that seemed to be his question as well.

All this time I hadn't wanted to turn back the cloth covering Lia's face but now I was forced to look at her, the two of us staring silently at her bruised features, her lank hair, her closed eyes. Her head was turned, as if she'd heard the rear door open and shifted her blind gaze to find out who had disturbed her, and I said, Oh Lia, and a sob burst from my throat.

Jim was swallowing repeatedly, the sound unnaturally loud, as if he had a tiny amplifier in his vocal cords, until he gripped me by both upper arms, so firmly I thought he was about to lift me from the ground. I don't even want to know, he said. Whatever it is? I just don't care.

He swiveled on his heel and returned to his truck, started it, and drove off.

I didn't wait, didn't even recover Lia's face, but instead shut the rear door and started up the van and drove off myself, moving quickly, less worried about a speed trap than the moment Jim would come to his senses and call the cops. I imagined the chase, the roadblock, the inevitable end. It wouldn't be so bad, probably, as Mrs. Stefanini would eventually get Lia back, but the publicity would wound her and I didn't want her to see Lia like this if I could help it. And I believed I could, even as I worried that each of the half-dozen or so late-model pickups that pulled in behind me over the next miles was Mads, about to track me down.

Once I got to the Mauckport Bridge I slowed, certain by then that Jim either hadn't called it in or had done so too late to matter; Indiana cops were powerless now, as the entire bridge was Kentucky's. Lia and I would make it, the cops wouldn't stop me, Mads couldn't find me.

My heart skipped when a Kentucky State Trooper, lights flashing, pulled a black van over on I-64, but the trooper didn't look up and I decided it was probably routine. Still, I'd been foolish to believe it would be easy—Kentucky had even more pickups—and for the next ten or fifteen miles, passing through Louisville's built-up waterfront and out again to the first suburbs, I seemed to be holding my breath. By the time I got to the Hapsburg Funeral Home, my stomach ached as if I'd been punched.

The front lot was three-quarters filled with cars, and in my tired state I took a few moments to realize they must have been in the middle of a funeral. *Not a good time*, I thought, and then, *No, it is*, and drove around back and parked and pressed the door buzzer.

The attendant, short and curly haired, wearing a blue surgical smock, his round face more freckles than skin, barely opened the door.

Mr. Hapsburg here? I asked.

He's in the middle of a service, he said. But I can find someone else to answer any questions.

No, I said, too tired to be anything but direct. I don't have any. Just get him. I promise, he won't be happy if you don't.

Maybe it was my disheveled appearance or the way I smelled or the unwavering nature of my voice, or simply the desire not to have to deal with someone who seemed so obviously off, but after a few seconds of waiting, a train horn sounding at a railroad crossing during the pause, he nodded.

The door clanked shut behind him and his footsteps disappeared and I stood waiting, determined not to think of what I was going to say to Mr. Hapsburg. My brain was fried and whatever I planned to say I'd no doubt forget by the time he came back, so instead I picked out patterns swirling through the brown paint before me, which soothed me: I only realized I'd heard steps returning down the long back hallway once the door was thrown open again. Mr. Hapsburg stood before me, looking elegant in his dark suit, a look undercut by his hands crossed in front of him, as if he worried I would kick him.

I wanted to, but I resisted the urge. I've got someone for you to take care of, I said.

He shifted from suspicious to solicitous. I'm sorry, he said. Did this just happen?

No. I glanced at the van. A few days ago. She was here and you let her go and now I've brought her back so you can fix her up.

You were here before, weren't you? he said, recognizing me. I didn't blame him for not doing so at first. When I'd last been here, I'd still had some semblance of normalcy. Now I looked half-dead and three-quarters crazy.

Yes, I said. I was. And I found the woman I was looking for.

Well, ma'am, he said. I'm sorry, I've forgotten your name, but this is highly unusual. There are protocols to follow, paperwork, things we have to do.

The attendant was behind him now, holding open the door.

Mr. Hapsburg, I said, you probably don't want him to hear what I'm going to tell you.

Over his shoulder, he said, Bobby? Shut that door, will you? There's a good boy.

Bobby did, but I didn't hear his footsteps disappearing, which meant he was listening in. *Fine by me*, I thought, and opened the van's back doors.

Oh my, he said, upon seeing Lia. Yes. She was here. No one's taken care of her, have they?

I have, I said. I'm taking care of her right now.

He stepped toward her and pulled aside the entire sheet. This is awful, he said. Who took her feet and ankles?

Don't, I said.

Don't what? he said, his voice imperious. Look here, miss, you've probably broken all kinds of laws.

And so have you, I said, and pulled out one of the Zanotti boots. Does this look familiar, I said? Or this, or this? I added, pulling out others. They should. They all came from bodies you embalmed and buried.

When he opened his mouth to protest I held up my hand. Amed Smith told me about your little racket, how you gloat that this is Kentucky and all kinds of women want to be buried in their riding boots, especially those who've never ridden. A hundred dollars a pair, isn't it? That's what you charge him?

His face was pale but he hadn't yet fully buckled, so I piled on. He even told me where the closet is that you keep them in. He hadn't, but Mr. Hapsburg wouldn't know that. Should we go in and see?

Or here, I said, and held up Amed's phone. Let's call the police. I'll wait. When they get here, I'll tell them about that closet. I might be in trouble, but you'll lose your business. What do you say?

He cleared his throat and said, Fine. What is it that you want?

His disdain didn't bother me; I wanted Lia taken care of. This is the deal, I said. You're going to embalm her. You're going to make her the best-looking corpse you've ever seen.

He shook his head. That won't be easy. The feet, for God's sake.

No one's going to be looking at her feet, I said. There are some Olivetti boots in there. They're hers. You'll put them on her and make them look like they're stuffed with great calves and feet.

You fool, he said. As you said, no one's going to look at her feet. But the body's not whole, and the embalming fluid will leak.

I'm aware of that, I said. I know the business. I also know that you can do a bang-up job making sure it doesn't happen, and that you will. You'll be the one massaging the body, making sure the fluid is properly distributed, you'll be the one making her up, you'll be the one washing her hair.

I flicked the phone on. It's five now. You can probably do a decent job in four hours, so I'll give you five to do a great one. When I come back at ten, we're going to call her family, and they're going to come down and see their daughter to say good-bye to her. Even if it's late, they'll want to come. Agreed? I said. Or should I start making phone calls?

His breath whistled through his long narrow nose. And if I do this?

If you do this, I'll forget all about the boots.

And how do I know you're telling the truth?

You don't, I said. But you haven't been for a long time either, so really, you can't say much about that.

He looked like he wanted to hit me, but I knew he wouldn't. Once you start bargaining you have hope, in this case hope that he might still get away with every bad thing he'd done. For all I knew, the boots were only the start of it.

All right, he said, and turned and knocked on the door. Bobby, get a gurney so we can get things going.

* * *

Home, I stripped off my clothes on the back porch and threw them in the trash and hurried inside to shower, sobbing with my head against the wall as the water poured over me. I hoped it would wash away the stink and the guilt and the agony, but it didn't seem to, not even after I scrubbed and shampooed and soaped and scrubbed again.

I cried until the water turned cold, and when I was shaking, I got out and wrapped myself in an oversized blue towel and sank onto the bed, intending to rest for only a moment. Lia had been so thin, thinner than I'd ever seen her, and I remembered her line whenever she looked at herself in the mirror before her period. *We could use an eating disorder.* Had she finally taken herself up on it? When I awoke it was nearly dark, the damp towel bunched uncomfortably beneath me, and something seemed wrong. *What?* I wondered, and heard Orlando crying outside my window, Amed's phone chirping beside me.

I ignored Orlando and grabbed for the phone, finding a picture frame instead—the picture of Lia and I at the beach together, which I had no memory of holding or looking at— the phone itself a little farther away on the tufted comforter.

A text message, from my own phone.

Come by, it said. *You have to. Please? Something really good has happened.*

I breathed deeply, gathering myself, and checked the timestamp. 8:02, five minutes ago, which meant I had time to get dressed, to comb my hair, to put on enough makeup to look presentable, to find suitable clothes for the funeral home. Time to stop in at Amed's on the way over too, since I wanted to tell him what the outcome had been, what he'd helped achieve. If he'd been a bastard, he'd earned that courtesy for helping me retrieve Lia.

I'd also have time to get ready to face Mrs. Stefanini for the first time in years, and perhaps the last. She would always hate me, but maybe now, for an hour or two, in addition to that hate, she would feel some warmth in my presence, know that I really had loved her family.

All right, I texted back. *Soon.*

And it took less time than I'd expected, probably because I knew that if I lingered, I'd find another thing wrong and another, only to end by convincing myself not to go through with it—would tell Mr. Hapsburg to call Mrs. Stefanini and be done with it—and I didn't want to be a coward. She should have her chance to say whatever she needed to me in person, and I should have the chance to say good-bye to Lia, regardless of what Mrs. Stefanini thought. If I waited even a day, I might be in jail, so I would go to see Amed in the spirit of general forgiveness.

* * *

I was outside his building just before nine and texted him, asking which apartment was his.

2B, came the immediate answer, as if he was watching me from the window. *Come on up.*

The old wooden stairs creaked beneath my heels and

there were no hall lights so I had to take my time in the dark. All right, Amed, I called out as I climbed. What's this good news? His door was open and I stepped in and stopped, stopped breathing too, it seemed. The hallway was dim, not dark, and Amed knelt at the end of it, his face battered, both eyes swollen shut, a bubble of blood emerging from one ruined nostril, which was how I knew he was alive.

My god, Amed, I said, noticing his right pinkie standing straight up from his splayed hand, an impossible angle. Who did this? I said.

I was about to kneel and attend to him when Mads, stepping out from behind the door, pushed it closed and said, Me. I did. He was enormous in the gloom, but the scariest thing was his white, incongruous smile.

He stepped toward me and palmed my head and said, You're next, and slammed my head against the wall.

17

When I came to I was sitting next to Amed on the floor, legs straight out before me, as if the two of us had been arranged, and my nose felt broken. I blew it into my palm.

Mads squatted next to me, thick fingers sorting through my purse. He pulled out a few things—a lipstick, my sunglasses case, which he opened and dropped back in, eye drops, a Swiss Army knife, which he pocketed, floss—then clicked it shut.

Is there a handkerchief in there? I said. Some tissues?

I held my hand out toward him when he glanced at me.

Wipe it on your blouse. That was my body, he said. She belonged to me.

I shook my head, which hurt. No, I managed to say, and then a little louder after I cleared my throat. She never belonged to you.

I paid for it. You shouldn't take what isn't yours. He slapped me across the ear, making my head ring. You got that?

When I didn't respond it wasn't from fear, though I was terrified, but because I worried that arguing would make him more dangerous. Amed still knelt, as if his knees and shins had been cemented to the floor, and the bruises on his face were darker. Soon his face would be as black as if he'd been burned. What would Mads do to me?

He seemed to read my mind. My body, he said. It's at a funeral parlor?

Talking felt like I was forming cinder blocks with my teeth and tongue, but eventually I said, Yes.

We'll get it back. He took a knife from his pocket, much larger than my Swiss Army one, and flicked it open it. This time of night, most of those places are empty.

Not tonight. He's waiting for me. Then I couldn't help it and started crying. It's my friend. He's fixing her up. Her mother's going to come by and see her.

Fixing her up? You mean embalming her? They're working on her? Someone's there? Shit, he said, and slammed the knife into the wooden floor. You really fucked yourself, you know that?

He backhanded Amed, who toppled over like a barrel and moaned.

I need a body, he said. A *female* body. He crab-walked a step closer and grabbed my chin and tilted my face up. You know what that means?

I've got a body, I said.

Exactly what I was thinking. A nice one, he said, freeing the knife from the floor. Perfect for what I need.

His thumb and fingers felt like they were about to

break bone. No, I said. I mean I have a body you can use. Female, the right age. A Jane Doe. We couldn't identify her.

Who's we?

The Danville coroner and me.

Danville? That's where she's at? Tricky, you coming up with that just when I needed it.

I didn't just come up with it, I said. She's been there almost six months.

Six months? So you'll have to bury her soon anyway, right? And you're thinking no one will miss her?

No, I said, pulling my feet under me and pushing myself upright against the wall. They'll miss her. My boss wants to find out who she is and get her back to her people. But he's pretty sure he won't be able to so, yes, he'll bury her next week.

For a long time he didn't say anything, just flipped the knife end over end in his hand, blade in his palm and then handle, blade and then handle. I couldn't look away. His eyes were so blue they seemed fake.

At last he stood and gripped the knife handle and slammed the knife into the wall between my legs, so close that it nicked one of my thighs. Was that blood trickling down my skin, or urine?

He leaned in and I felt his warm breath on my cheek. Just so we're clear? he said. If you're lying to me? He pressed one hand to my stomach and slid it slowly over my crotch to the knife, making my skin crawl with a thousand roaches. Then he jimmied it side to side, pressing its blade against me. Next time I do this? It'll be a foot higher and twice as deep.

* * *

Come here, Mads said, standing by the sink. Get that water bottle from his trash can and fill it up and cap it. After I had, he said, Put the bottle in your purse and then go on into the bathroom.

Why? I said, my legs beginning to shake.

Because you're going to use the bathroom. I'm tired of you pissing yourself. I want your bladder empty.

I don't have to go.

He held the knife toward me. You do, and you will. Leave the door open.

So I did. I felt him watching me the whole time but I wouldn't give him the satisfaction of looking up. When I was done, I washed my hands, as if this was entirely normal. His pocket was glowing, from a phone. Mine, I thought, since he'd texted me on it.

If that's mine, I said, I should probably answer it. They're looking for me.

He pulled the phone out. Who's Joan?

My probation officer. If I don't answer, she'll get the cops after me.

That's your problem, he said.

It'll be yours too if I go down to Danville and one of them stops me.

They won't know where you are.

Amed's van? I thought of Jim. They're probably looking for that too.

You won't be in Amed's van, he said. You think I'm

going to let you go down there yourself? You'd go right to the police.

I wouldn't, I swear. I give you my word.

Yes, he said. And fish have fur. Not to worry. You'll have company the whole way. I'm not fucking stupid. And we're taking my truck.

He pulled a blue bandana from his pocket and wiped down the front doorknob. Then he stood by the door for a few seconds, listening, before opening it and peeking out into the darkened hallway.

All right, he said, pushing the door open. Even near a whisper, his gravelly voice was loud. Stand in the hall. I'm going to close the door for a minute, no more. When I open it, you're going to be right there. If you've moved at all, if you try to run, if you start to yell, I'll catch you and kill you. Got it?

I nodded.

He didn't move aside and I had to brush against him as I passed, which I knew was intentional. He wanted me to breathe in his sweat, his stink, to mark me like an animal. When I was in position he held up a single crooked finger and said, One minute. Do not move. With his hand still in the bandana he started to close the door. Put your fingers in your ears, he said. You're not going to want to hear this.

I did and closed my eyes, my heart pounding, feeling dizzy and beginning to sway in the dark, thinking I should run. Yet I didn't, hearing Lia's voice say over and over, *It's not real it's not real it's not real*, trying to calm me, even as I knew she was wrong. It *was* real. The dead have no grasp of the truth, and just as I made my mind up to flee, Mads tapped my elbow. I opened my eyes and unplugged my ears and he wiped down the doorknob on this side and said, Let's go.

* * *

The floor of his pickup was covered with balled-up papers and old beer bottles, crushed cans. Put your seatbelt on, he said. I don't want anyone stopping us for anything. When I had my seatbelt on, he reached across and locked the door.

After a few minutes of winding through the nearly empty city streets, he had us headed east on 64, the speedometer floating at 65. Cars passed us and he began to whistle. When we passed Blankenbaker Lane and the overhead lights stopped and we got into a rhythm of the tires thrumming over the expansion joints every quarter mile, I began to feel a bit safer in the dark. Not safe, really, but maybe bolder, or simply desperate to survive, and I said, I don't believe you.

Don't believe what?

That you killed Amed. That's what you want me to think. All that drama back at his apartment, that little show of wiping down door handles and having me stop up my ears so I wouldn't hear you slit his throat? That's what you want, isn't it? For me to think you're fucking crazy?

He didn't respond, which was worse. I wanted him to talk, because talking kept the horror at bay; horror was always worse, disembodied. And saying anything was better than picturing Amed gasping out his last breaths, drowning in his own blood with no one there to comfort him. And later, no one to protect him.

I bit my lip, hard enough to draw blood, not wanting to give Mads the satisfaction of seeing me crumble. He must have intuited my struggle, because at last he did speak.

Believe what you want, he said. He reached across and popped the glove compartment open and pulled out a pistol, which he set on his lap. The sweet licorice scent of its oil filled the truck. But here's something else for you to believe. You cause me any problems? I'll kill you and anyone you involve. Whatever happened to Amed is already on you. He wouldn't have gone to French Lick if it wasn't for you, but I don't care any more than I'll care who else gets caught up in this. You can believe in the tooth fairy if you want, but I'm getting that body. Every one of those doctors is going to go home from that conference a happy camper. Now shut up and let me drive. I prefer to travel in silence.

* * *

And all the ninety dark miles to Danville through sparse traffic and lonely looking farms glowing on distant hills, past hulking dark churches and clogged and brightly lighted liquor stores, he didn't say a word. I didn't think he would kill me, if he planned to, until we'd got McDonald's body in his truck, as he wouldn't want to do all that lifting by himself, so for a while, I thought about smacking my head against the window to knock myself out, or unbuckling my seatbelt and unlocking the door and tumbling onto the highway, or shifting around and kicking him in the head and making him crash. But none of those would work, I knew, so instead I occupied myself with the pleasing fantasy that Mr. Hapsburg had called Mrs. Stefanini when I didn't show, that she'd rushed to the funeral parlor and seen her daughter at last.

I doubted Mr. Hapsburg would tell her I'd had any part in it, which shouldn't have mattered, but it did. I wanted her to know I'd protected Lia, to be able, finally, to begin to forgive me, but it wasn't going to happen. Not now, not ever. I turned toward the window to cry.

South of Harrodsburg Mads began asking questions about the morgue and its layout, whether or not it had alarms, getting directions. I took him through Danville's deserted four-street downtown with its lighted-up war memorial and hanging petunia baskets, past the federal building and hospital, though it wasn't the most direct route, hoping some cop or stray passerby would notice my panic-stricken face. No luck. Eventually I steered him past the elementary school where Mads read aloud the signboard: READERS ARE LEADERS.

Then we were in the lot behind the morgue. Mads parked as far away as possible from the lone light burning over the back door and turned the truck off and lowered his window and we sat for a long time, Mads staring into his side-view mirror as we both listened to the deep hum of cicadas and katydids, to summer in the South, to the wind gusting through the leaves of the big oaks and maples in the nearby yards where huge branches had come down in the recent storms, and, twice, to the hoot of a distant train.

Finally, I said, What are we waiting for?

Shut up, he said.

The air smelled of tar, some newly resurfaced road. After another train passed, closer from the sound of its whistle, he turned the truck on and drove a half mile up the street, parking this time in the half-empty lot of a tire store, keeping his window open all the while.

You smell, you know that? he said.

I did—sweat and fear and something darker, something older, something more animal; what was human was disappearing. A few minutes later a cop car cruised slowly down the street and Mads didn't even have to tell me not to move, though I thought of reaching over and hitting the horn. I didn't, because I didn't know if it worked, and I didn't yell out the opened window either and the cop never once looked around.

When his taillights disappeared around a corner Mads started up his truck and pulled into the morgue lot again, backing the truck to the morgue's rear door.

We've got at least fifteen minutes, he said. More than enough time. One of those keys on your key ring will get us in?

I said it would.

Good. He titled the gun into the light, where it flashed blue and silver and the licorice scent of its oil seemed to intensify. You know what a bullet does in water?

Sure. It slows down.

That's right, he said, conversationally. But it does other things too. Last time I used this gun? I had a man fill his mouth with water. Didn't let him swallow. Stuck the gun in his mouth and told him not to worry. That even if I pulled the trigger it wouldn't kill him, because of the water. Slowing things down, you know?

He looked over to make sure I was paying attention. I was.

Thing is, he said, I lied. I don't know the science of it, but that water? When I pulled the trigger, it did something to that bullet, multiplied its force. His head just *exploded*. So, here's what we're going to do. He tucked the gun into the back of his pants and sat back and said, You're going to unlock that door and let us in and we're going to get the body and put her in back and get out of here. No one is going to find us. No one is going to hear an alarm, silent or otherwise, and no one is going to show up. If they do, I'll pour half the bottle of water into their mouth and shoot them and save the other half for you. Got it?

Unable to speak, my body frozen, I nodded.

Good. Then let's go. And be quick about it. If that cop doesn't find his donut shop open, he might be back sooner than we expect.

But it wasn't the cops who showed up unexpectedly, just as I reached to unlock the door and long before any alarm could have been triggered. It was Buddy.

18

Did you get the call too, Elena? he asked, obviously surprised to see me. He hadn't noticed Mads yet.

What call? I said, hoping that my pained expression, my tremulous voice, would convince him to leave.

The body in Henry Jackson Park. Been there a bit. Decomposed.

He was here for his tools, then. Good thing is, he went on, fumbling with his jangling keys, doesn't seem to be a murder, so we don't have to worry about that.

Buddy, why don't you just head out there? You won't need your tools.

How do you know that? he said.

She doesn't, Mads said, coming up behind him. She just wants you to go.

I closed my eyes, so I didn't see if Buddy's expression changed from surprise to puzzlement to anger, but his voice told me that's what had happened.

Who are you?

The guy you shouldn't ever have seen, Mads said.

I opened my eyes when I heard him cock the pistol. The keys went still in Buddy's hand and he seemed to have stopped breathing, his face to have aged years.

Now look here, mister, he said. We don't have any drugs, nothing you could use anyway. And certainly no money.

You can let him go, I said to Mads, careful not to use Buddy's name. He doesn't have a good memory.

What? Buddy said. What are you talking about, Elena?

Good or not, he's still got one, Mads said. Let's take this inside.

Elena, Buddy said. What's going on?

Mads pressed the gun to Buddy's head and pushed. Open the door, he said.

The tang of urine filled the air and a dark stain bloomed on Buddy's pants, accompanied by the awful feeling that the worst thing I'd done to Buddy was to cause the look of shame spreading now across his face.

It was atrocious, that shame, and me its source. Each day it seemed I forged new links on the chain of my crimes, despite my best intentions, and the worst of them never to be judged, at least as long as my soul dragged around this tired body. But I could judge myself, and I did.

Oh Buddy, I said. I'm so sorry.

Not your fault, Elena, he said, and stepped forward and sorted through the keys until he had the right one. His trembling hands made sliding it in difficult.

Stop stalling, Mads said, glancing around for the circling cop.

I'm not, Buddy said. I'm nervous, okay? Just give me a second.

And then he had it. Wait, Mads said, grabbing his arm. She told me something about an alarm. What kind is it?

Sweat dripped from Buddy's nose, or was that a tear? In the dim yellow light I couldn't tell. He seemed to want to turn and look at me, to try and guess what I'd said, but Mads kept the gun pressed to the back of his head.

At last Buddy cleared his throat and said, We don't have one.

Good, Mads said, and pulled the gun back. That's what she said. Let's go.

* * *

Inside, Buddy's hand went to the wall, searching for the lights, but Mads cracked his forearm with the gun.

No lights, he said. No reason to let anyone else know we're here.

Fuck, Buddy said, gripping his arm. You could have just told me.

I just did. Now stop wasting time.

The hallway was easy to navigate because of the light over the door, but once we moved into the morgue proper it was impossible to see, even after pausing to let our eyes adjust. I could feel Buddy thinking, imagining ways to overpower someone with a gun. *Not going to happen,* I thought, and hoped he picked up on it. *Maybe if we didn't cause any problems he'd just let us go in the end.* That wasn't true either.

Buddy spoke first. Listen. This is nuts. I need some kind of light or I'll knock everything over. And I don't even know what you want.

Easy, Mads said. I'm here for the body, the one you're about to bury.

McDonald's? I heard the wonder in his voice. What do you want with her?

Mads pulled a small flashlight from his pocket and clicked it on, shone the light on the floor before us. Just take me to her, he said.

This way, I said, and started out, Buddy following behind, Mads off to the side so the flashlight beam swayed in front of my shoes. I thought Buddy tugged my blouse but I couldn't be sure, and even if he had I didn't know how to respond, so I kept moving.

The air grew cooler as we descended and I thought how pleasurable that often felt, these recent dog days of summer. When I hadn't known I was actually happy. Why do we only learn of these things too late?

I stepped onto the flashlight beam.

Move over, Mads said.

You move over, I said.

He did, which surprised me. A step later he swore and dropped the light.

Fuck, he said, and squatted to grab it, came back up swearing again and flashing it at us. What the fuck was that?

He pressed one hand to his head and moved his hand into the light. I'm fucking bleeding.

He swung the light back to the wall, the row of nails

sticking out, Buddy's white lab coat on the third one, my blue one on the fourth.

Fuck, he said. Did you do that on purpose?

I screwed my eyes shut and turned my head away when he shone the light in my eyes.

Do what on purpose? I said. All I'm doing is walking. Put that off me, will you? I'll be blind otherwise. Which in truth was what I'd hoped would happen to him, one of the nails scratching his eye, debilitating him. No such luck.

Good, Mads said. Maybe then you'll cut yourself too. Fuck! This *hurts*.

I caught Buddy looking at me but didn't return his glance, sure Mads would pick up on it. Mads kicked me in the leg so hard I gasped.

Stop it, Buddy said. There's no reason to kick her just because you can't watch where you're walking.

Mads swung the flashlight beam to Buddy's face; Buddy squinted and turned away. Got nothing to say now, do you? Mads said. Now go.

Buddy was in front of me. I stumbled on my first step, stuck my hand out for balance, reached into Buddy's baggy right pocket. Swiftly I felt around, hoping for a knife or a scalpel, something useful from all the things he usually tucked in there, but felt only an apple and something long and smooth and nearly flat, like a deodorant stick. I grabbed it all the same, slipping it into a pocket with one hand while steadying myself against the wall with the other.

Move, Mads said loudly.

I'm trying, I said, breathing in sharply. But that kick almost broke my leg.

Next one will.

We were at the cooler and I said, She's in the third drawer, and Mads told me to pull her out and when I did he yanked back the covering sheet. Fuck, he said.

What? Buddy said.

You didn't tell me she'd been autopsied.

You didn't ask, I said. Besides, it won't matter. They can still practice on her.

No shit, Sherlock, he said. But it's not the same thing. Blood was dripping into his eye and he wiped it off with the tail of his shirt.

Who can work on her? Buddy said. What's this about?

Mads didn't answer and I wasn't going to—the less Buddy knew, the better—and for a few seconds it was just the three of us there breathing, looking down at McDonald's sunken abdomen, the brutal postmortem Y incised in her body.

Then Mads said, Fuck it, she'll have to do, and told us to bring her out.

No, Buddy said. Not until you tell me what's going on.

Before Mads could hit him—I was certain he was about to—I said, Buddy, don't. Please? Just trust me on this? It's better, okay?

This is all tied up with whatever you wouldn't tell me about, isn't it? he said. You've gone back to wrangling corpses? Is that it? I'm surprised, Elena, he said. I really am. I thought you'd changed.

Yes, I said, wanting to shut him up. I'm sorry. I thought I had too.

Better he think that than keep asking questions.

Fine, he said. You two can have her. The faster you're out of my life the better.

So we wheeled her down the hallway to the rear door and lifted her off the gurney and hoisted her into Mads's camper while Mads stood watch beside us, wrist pressed to his bloody forehead.

Good, he said. Put the gurney back, just inside the door.

Buddy did, the wheels rattling over the saddle, and Mads shut the door and locked it.

Now get in the truck, Mads said.

Both of us? Buddy asked.

Just you, he said.

This is crazy, Buddy said. Sorry. Won't do it.

You will, Mads said. Or I can start shooting right here.

Buddy opened his mouth to say something, thought better of it, and began to climb in. When he ducked his head to clear the doorway Mads clubbed him behind the ear with the gun and Buddy fell forward onto McDonald's, sprawling across her.

I tried to climb in behind him. Fuck no, Mads said. You ride up front with me.

Well, at least let me cover them up. It seems wrong, leaving them like that.

Not a chance. He searched through Buddy's pockets and found his cellphone, shut the camper door and locked it, and said, All right. Let's go.

* * *

I wasn't surprised at the blood; head wounds often look worse than they are. He wiped it with his shirtsleeve but it kept flowing, so he pulled out his bandana and pressed it to the cut. Uselessly, after a few minutes.

Fuck, he said, wadding up the soaked bandana and tossing it aside. You got any maxi pads with you?

No.

Well you better fucking find something or I'll take it out on you.

I went through my pockets and came up with the tube I'd found in Buddy's pocket. Camphor rub. How about this? I said, and handed it to him.

He held it close to his face and read the label, glancing up to watch the road.

Alcanfor? What the hell is that? Is it safe?

Yeah, it's safe, I said and took it from him and popped the top and rubbed it heavily on my forearm, over my fleur-de-lis tattoo.

Stinks, he said.

It's what they make mothballs out of.

You want me to rub mothballs on my face?

I don't care what you do.

How'd you get it?

Buddy and I always carry it, in case we work on a decomposing body. Masks the smell. Especially important with floaters.

Never seen it before.

Your pharmacy cater to Hispanics?

No, he said. Rub it on your lip, he said. Your cut.

I wasn't bleeding anymore, but I didn't tell him that—he'd slap me again to open it up if I did—and though it stung I knew nothing bad would come of it.

He watched me and took it and said, If this fucking makes it worse, or if it hurts like a bastard, I'm going to open up your forehead too.

It'll hurt, I said. But not too bad. Press hard. That cut's pretty big. You need a lot to stop any bleeding.

Two minutes after he rubbed it on, the bleeding stopped.

See? I said. It's a counterirritant.

He laughed. Feels good, actually. Cooling.

* * *

For a long time nothing happened. We passed several cars and a lot more passed us. Three AM was a couple of hours too early for tractors to be on the highway, clogging traffic, so I kept a lookout for a static parked roadside, lights out to catch speeders, but the only one I saw was on the other side of the divide ten miles south of Frankfort. Then we were headed west on 64 toward Louisville and Mads kept to the right lane, meaning I couldn't even cast terrified glances at passing drivers. I was sweating rivers, my back, thighs, and underarms. *Oh God oh God oh God*, I kept thinking, but if He was there He wasn't listening. No flat tires, no miraculously appearing flashing lights, no accident to slow traffic and give me the chance to jump.

The end was coming and there was nothing I could do about it. A lump grew in my throat, for all the times during the scandal I'd wished I was dead. And then I found a kind of peace, observing myself as if from far above, as if my body—whatever it had been to me through all the years, about to be nothing but parts—was someone else's. I witnessed the pain it felt, in the leg, the head, the lip, the way it shifted away from the gigantic man beside it on the old bench seat, what a beautiful thing it was, how useful.

19

Near Louisville hope surged again; traffic, a flat tire from construction debris, something would go my way. I remembered Dr. Weaver's patient, giving up a few moments early. *That won't be me,* I thought. But the roads were mostly empty—a few truckers, a few teens dragging in souped-up tiny cars, a few tired men and women heading home from late shifts or off to work at early ones, and none of them even glanced in my direction. Nor did any of the UPS drivers steering their big rigs toward the airport. No cops, no construction, no traffic lights at all. We were speeding toward the bridge, toward Indiana, toward our inevitable end, and once we reached Mads's trailer, not a power on earth could reach us, not in time.

Mads wasn't merciful. He'd drag it out, probably, enjoy watching us beg, so I found myself hoping for prison. For Buddy it was different; he could go back to a good life, and that thought made me slip into despair. I checked my watch, and already we were an hour and a half into the drive, an hour and a half closer to Mads's, and I had no illusions about what awaited us there. He wouldn't let us live, how could he? I felt myself panicking, about to break down and ask him to spare us, but I fought it, knowing he'd lie.

So I prayed for a swift end, some poison, perhaps, a little cyanide mist, which would dissipate quickly and leave no trace. He could use the bodies then; he'd have plenty of blank death certificates he could falsify. Thinking about it at a clinical remove, thrusting myself back into my old life, made it easier to bear and kept me from focusing on worse alternatives, rape before being shot or strangled, our compromised bodies shipped to his brother's crematorium, not even used for parts, our ashes dumped in some polluted stream.

* * *

Downtown Louisville was both deserted and lighted-up, looking like a stage set awaiting its early morning actors. Garbage, news and coffee trucks, sleepy factory workers, road graders and dump trucks and their chattering crews. I knew what an hour would bring, sunlight gilding the skyscrapers, the blue-shadowed streets below beginning to awaken, had witnessed it thousands of times without ever once contemplating its miraculous nature. I ached for the chance, just once more, to smell the diesel exhaust of the day's first buses.

Mads bounced in his seat, as if to keep himself awake.

Tired? I asked, trying to dampen the hope sparking in my breast. I couldn't bear to be disappointed again, I'd crumble if I were.

Hungry, he said. Haven't eaten all day. Another thing you fucked up for me.

I can drive for a while, I said.

Right. Like I'm going to let that happen.

Right, I said. I've got big plans to escape you.

You might not have any plans, he said. But you're still hoping. Everyone does, right up until the end.

You've done this before? I said.

No denial from him, no bragging; either might have been more reassuring.

Then the lighted city was behind us, the dark river running down to our right, and his bouncing stopped and I felt foolish for allowing myself to hope. But after another mile, only two or three from the bridge, he shook his head like a dog and began to wheeze. Hot in here, he said, opening his window. Warm air streamed in.

I switched on the radio.

Knock it off, he said, and reached to turn it off, but his hand hit the dashboard too hard.

He squinted, leaned forward as if the windshield had grown dirty, grew unsteady on the accelerator; we sped up, slowed down, began to swerve.

If this is going to happen, I thought, *let it happen before we're on the bridge.*

As I thought it, we rounded the broad curve toward the bridge much too fast, Mads swinging the truck into the far lane, and I screamed, thinking that we'd slam into the abutment or hit the railing with enough speed that we'd ride up over it and be launched into the air, crashing on the bank and being crushed, or, worse, splashing into the river to drown. Or that we'd roll over and all be killed, my own end mirroring Lia's.

At the last second Mads swerved right again, crossing both lanes and banging into the guardrail before straightening out; my head slammed against the window.

What the fuck did you do to me? he said. Why are we going so slow? He fumbled for the gun, which slid from his lap onto the floorboards.

You're going to start hallucinating soon, I said. Having seizures. Pull over before it's too late.

You fucking bitch, he said, and slapped me, but his arm strength was gone; it was like being struck with a Kleenex.

I grabbed the wheel and yanked it toward me, slamming us once more into the guardrail as Mads tried uselessly to pull it back. He still had some foot control and stomped down on the accelerator, the truck lurching forward and throwing off sparks, gaining on the car in front of us. Just before we hit it, Mads began to gurgle and convulse and his foot came off the accelerator, and after another ten yards of metal screeching against metal and ten more of the front tire riding up the guardrail, we slid at last to a stop, the car in front of us heading blithely on its way.

Mads was still convulsing, his arms slamming against my hands holding the wheel, but once I let go, the convulsions stopped just as suddenly as they'd begun.

I didn't trust that he wasn't acting. For a few seconds I leaned against the far door, watching him, then reached out and poked him. When I got no reaction I slapped him, and then again, harder, and finally had to make myself stop, as I wanted to go on beating him forever. Then I reached under his legs and felt around the floor for the gun, grabbed it, turned the truck off, took the keys from the ignition, and rolled down my window and climbed out.

Buddy was banging on the camper door.

Jesus, he said, when I opened it. What happened? Are you all right?

Camphor poisoning, I said, and filled him in on the details, how the body absorbs it through open cuts but not skin, how swiftly it turns toxic in the blood.

Is he dying?

No. He'll come to from the seizure in an hour, and he'll need medical help in the next three.

Buddy laughed with relief. Well it won't take that long for the cops to get here. We can call them.

No Buddy, I said. We can't.

Why not?

A car slowed as it passed, the driver taking us in, me with the gun in my hand and Buddy disheveled and gesticulating, and as he sped off I said, I'll explain once we're moving. Let's just get him in the back first.

With McDonald's? he said.

Either that or he rides with us.

Okay, fine, he said, moving to the driver's door. But this better be good.

* * *

Some of it I made up as we drove, some of it I didn't tell him, all of it was true. That I hadn't been wrangling corpses, that I was searching for my oldest friend's body, that I'd found her and planned to return her to her mother, that doing so meant I'd had to break probation and that now I would have to go to prison, that psychotic Mads had tracked me down, that McDonald's was meant to save me, that I'd never expected Buddy to become involved. That I needed a few last favors from him, in order to escape, to have a life, a second one.

But Elena, he said, don't be foolish. The cops will understand, I'm sure of it.

They can understand all they want, I said. That doesn't mean they won't have to do their job, the cops and the lawyers and the judge. But even if they do and let me go, my life really isn't a life. Please, I said. This will be a chance.

We crossed over into Indiana, exited the highway and circled under the bridge and came back up around and were crossing it now the other way, on the lower portion of the span. The river, restless and full, glistened black beneath us in the blue light of dawn. Soon we'd be speeding through Louisville, heading toward Danville, and soon after that we'd be at my exit, but Buddy hadn't decided yet. And then when we reached the Kentucky shore he did.

What did you say the nurses will need to give him for the seizures?

Thank you, Buddy, I said, and gripped his knobby hand on the wheel. Can you let me off at home?

Yes, he said. But don't thank me yet. I'm not sure how this is all going to work.

Benzodiazepine for the seizures. Tell them to watch him for another four hours. After that he'll come around. He'll be hallucinating. He may say something about a woman in his truck. About me. But most likely he won't remember anything from the last day or so. Everything will be a blur. That will work in your favor.

How? Buddy asked, looking at me longer than seemed safe, studying my face.

Whatever he says won't matter, I said. You say you were at the morgue to get your supplies and he jumped you. Later it will come out that I'd told Amed about McDonald's, that's how he knew about her body, and he's always after bodies. You'll have Mads's gun. That's all you'll need to prove he's a liar.

My DNA will be in the back of the camper, yours in the truck.

You helped put McDonald's back there, and who knows what he'll have done with me. I left a note behind when I was in his trailer. They'll search it, find bodies and the note, wonder what happened to me. They'll probably think he took me to his brother's and burned me up.

And the three hours during which I didn't show up to get the body at Henry Jackson Park?

He knocked you out with the gun once he began to feel symptoms of the poison. But you got lucky. You came to before he did and made the call.

And you, he said, hitting his blinker for the exit. What

will become of you? You're just going to walk away from your house, your life?

It's a house, Buddy. Not a home. You know that. Please, Buddy. This is the only way.

He didn't say a thing until we got to the end of the drive, where he pulled over and shifted into park and sat rocking in his seat, his face cupped in his hands.

Through his fingers, his voice was thick and muffled. I don't know, Elena, he said. I just don't know about any of it.

I leaned close to him. Buddy, do you want me to go to prison?

He looked at me, his eyes tried and moist. Of course not. But I don't want to either. I can't keep the story straight as it is.

That's a good sign, I said. The police always suspect people who have good stories. You were hit on the head, and you're going to have trouble remembering a lot of things.

I pushed the creaking door open. After I stepped out and shut the door, I stood looking at him. It never works, but I was trying to fix him forever in my memory. I'll be back with the cat in five minutes, I said.

On the way up the driveway, I smelled gasoline and wet cut grass; only dawn, and already my neighbors were getting on with their lives. I wanted to be able to too.

* * *

Six minutes, I said when I returned. Sorry.

Orlando was a peculiar cat, always liking to drive. I slipped him in the open window and he began purring right way, sitting up tall enough to see over the dash.

This is nuts, Buddy said.

I didn't want to break down, so I said, Remember, Buddy, bury McDonald's. You don't have to reclassify her now, since I'll be out of the picture. I never sent the changed autopsy findings to anyone else. The mayor will have to live with the murder rate going up on his watch, and McDonald's still might be identified sometime. But get rid of Carmine Semple's missing person's report. Put it somewhere no one will ever find it. If you do, no one will be looking for her, and I can take her name.

You said favors, Buddy said. Carmine Semple is one. What else?

I'd put the cat in the truck before telling him. Somehow I thought that would make it harder for him to refuse me. Shitty, I knew, but this time, at least, I was manipulating the living to guard the dead, not to strip them. I cleared my throat.

It's Amed, I said. His body. He's all alone in his apartment. Do you think you could drive there and sit with him, call the cops? Say that everything with you and Mads happened there? I hate to think of him left like that. Defenseless.

My god, he said. You're really something.

I had to hurry. Wait, I said. I thought I heard something. I went to the back and opened the camper. Mads was still unconscious. From my purse I pulled the handkerchief-wrapped hand and placed it next to his, as if he was reaching for it. Lifting it from the cooler in my basement hadn't been easy; though it weighed only a pound, I'd had a sudden fear of touching it. Peculiar, as I'd handled bodies and their parts for a decade and a half, but now, the hand seemed almost like a holy relic. And looking at it near the still-unconscious bulk of Mads, I thought better of it and tucked the hand under a tarp; the police would find it when they searched the back. What would happen then I wasn't sure, but at least there was the possibility it could be traced, returned to a grieving family with the rest of someone's remains.

When I came back, Buddy had made up his mind, which my little delay had been designed to accomplish. His essential decency was something I aspired to.

He shook his head, but he said, I never wanted a cat. God knows how it'll work out.

You'll make it work, Buddy. I know you. I gave him Amed's address, directions, and then I said, I want to thank you. For everything. I promise I'll let you know how I am.

You better, he said, shifting the truck into drive. You goddamn well better.

20

A month later the obituary appeared in the Danville *Advocate Messenger*, a few brief words. *Jane Doe, midthirties, an apparent homicide. Because of her tattoo, identified only as McDonald's. No known survivors. Interred in Bellevue Cemetery. The queen is dead,* it said. *Long live the queen.* I clicked on the accompanying ad and sent flowers to the grave anonymously.

I thought of adding a message on the condolences page, something about how up here in New York water from the faucet is cold enough to make my teeth ache, how fall comes weeks earlier—trees beginning to burn red and orange in mid-September, the crisp afternoon air, sweater weather— or about success and sorrow, but I figured that would be too much. I also didn't write Dr. Handler, though I was tempted to. She'd announced U of L's new willed-body program: 100 percent Informed Consent, and she said she did so in honor of Amed, that he'd come to her with that suggestion shortly before he died, that it was yet another step in the university's ongoing process of protecting the dead. *We will no longer accept transients' bodies*, she said. *Or those unclaimed at the medical examiner's office.* It was a lovely gesture, but as far as she knew, as far as anyone in the city could tell, I'd been Ricky Mads's last victim, my final whereabouts unknown. To them, Elena Kelly was a ghost, and a ghost she would remain.

Which was why I'd never contacted Mrs. Stefanini either. I ached to tell her I'd done everything I could to bring Lia home, that driven by the desire to lessen her pain, I'd been scared but dogged, that I was proud I'd eventually succeeded, but all I could hope was that she knew. That Mr. Hapsburg or the police had told her, that she'd guessed. And if she hadn't? Lia was home and mostly whole, Mrs. Stefanini had her daughter back, and, in comparison, an unchanged opinion of me was immaterial. A thought I consoled myself with often.

For now I had a bit of my savings left, a new name that I answered to as if it had always been my own, a new apartment, a job as a waitress in a ferned café. And on my wall, dozens of pictures. Pictures of Lia, pictures of Lia and me, of the two of us holding our minty drinks out to the warming sun, of us smiling at the Derby and in front of tobacco barns and high up on the state fair Ferris wheel, smiling in the belief that the future we plunged toward was ours. Old friends, I'd tell whoever was my first visitor, one of them was my sister, I'd say. From long ago, so long ago it seems another life.

ACKNOWLEDGEMENTS

Many thanks to Nicole Aragi for her years of unwavering support and tireless advocacy. Thanks also to my editor Dan Smetanka, who improved the book at every turn. And thanks too to the superb team at Counterpoint/Soft Skull, who have been an absolute pleasure to work with: Rolph Blythe, Megan Fishmann, Corinne Kalasky, and Kelly Winton.

Greatest thanks of all to my wife Anne. EWTBTB.